His For A Week:
BOUGHT

EM BROWN

His For A Week:
BOUGHT

CHAPTER ONE

*I*s *he fucking serious?* Ben communicated via a stare to his cousin. But Jason Lee, having thrown down a few shots of scotch from a bottle of Macallan Rare Cask, was too intoxicated for nonverbal communication.

"It's the best, dude," seconded Derek, who sat across the booth from Ben in the latest of many trendy restaurants to open up in San Francisco's SOMA district.

With a frown, Ben turned his gaze back to Jake Whitehurst, who sported a salacious grin as he swirled the scotch in his shot glass. Almost immediately, Ben hadn't liked Jake. Something in the guy's smug expression and the need to comment about the price of his Rolex watch ($12,000) and his shades from Cartier ($1,700) had left Ben less than impressed. Not that Ben begrudged the guy his haute couture when he himself had recently dropped two thousand for Louis Vuitton shades and gifted his mother a Tiffany bracelet that cost more than most mid-sized cars, but he never felt the need to brag about it.

If it weren't for the fact that Jake was Jason's friend

and former college roommate, and Ben's father wanted Jake's business connections, Ben would have called it a night. He had tried to be cordial most of the evening, but Jake's most recent revelation pushed his tolerance to the brink.

"You so hard up to get a date you have to *buy* one?" he asked Jake.

"Getting a date the old-fashioned way is too much fucking work," Jake scoffed.

Ben was incredulous. Jake was a good-looking guy in his mid-twenties. And, thanks to the successful sports agency his dad had founded, the bastard was rich. That took a man further than even his looks. A man could be as ugly as a naked mole rat, but money made him pretty.

"Women these days think they're so special," Jack continued. "But at the Scarlet Auction, you see what you like, you make a bid, an hour later, the girl's yours."

Ben raised his brows. "Girl?"

"You know what I mean. They're not underage or anything. Just single, hot, and ready to get banged."

"But some of them look like they could be, you now, teens," Derek chortled.

"That's gross," Ben replied, referring to both the idea of going out with jailbait and the way Derek practically *giggled.*

"Oh, come on, don't tell me you don't fantasize about banging a high school cheerleader, with their short little skirts and cute little pom-poms."

"I've been with high school cheerleaders — in high school. So no, I don't fantasize about them anymore."

The other three broke into guffaws. Jason clapped Ben on the back and slurred, "'Cause you're an old man now." Jason lowered his voice conspiratorially. "He turned *thirty* last year."

"I turned thirty and I still fantasize about high school cheerleaders," Derek said.

Because you never got within ten feet of one, Ben couldn't resist thinking.

Jason patted Ben's shoulder. "Just messin' with you, cuz." He looked across the table at Derek and Jake. "Honestly, there isn't a chick this guy couldn't get. Even in kindergarten, Ben was the *man*."

"Bet having the Lee family name didn't hurt," Jake said, unable to keep the envy out of his tone.

"Hey, dude, you related to Bruce Lee?" Derek asked.

An accomplished martial artist, Ben could have said he had that in common with the kung-fu legend, but there were no family ties that he was aware of. Instead, Ben replied, "Your last name's Nixon. Does that mean you're related to Richard Nixon?"

"The Scarlet Auction only happens once a month. Bidding starts at midnight tonight," Jake said. "We can all get dates for our week at the lake."

Ben's jaw tightened at the thought of spending the next several days at Jake's cabin, but Jason had assured him the best way to do business with Jake was to socialize with him.

"I don't need an auction to get a date," Ben said.

Jake shook his head. "I don't want yours to be the odd girl out. Either get a girl at the Scarlet Auction or come stag."

"Don't worry. They're not ugly chicks," Derek added. "The women who run the auction are very selective, so you're guaranteed to walk away with a hot one, dude."

Ben stared at Derek and briefly wondered if a kick to the guy's head would stop him from talking like a surfer out of an '80s beach flick.

Jason put an arm around Ben. "Come on, cuz. You don't want to be the only one at the lake without female companionship."

"Yeah, 'companionship,'" snickered Jake as he threw back a shot and motioned for the server to bring the tab.

Ben made no reply at first. He didn't want to "buy" a date at this Scarlet Auction. Hell, he couldn't imagine bringing any woman, bought or otherwise, to hang out with these wankers for a week in a remote lakeside cabin.

On the other hand, due to his rigorous traveling schedule on behalf of expanding the family's real estate empire, he hadn't had *female companionship* in more than three weeks. There was the waitress in Berlin and the singer in Phuket, but the sex had been vanilla and barely enough to keep his balls from going blue.

As if reading his mind, Derek said, "And at the

auction, you get girls who are into the kinky stuff."

Ben couldn't help but perk up.

"Yeah, ever since *Fifty Shades of Grey*, all girls are into that shit," Jake said. "I don't even bother with girls who aren't."

"How does the Scarlet Auction work?" Ben asked.

"You make a bid, you sign a contract, and the girl's yours for a week. At the end of the week, you part ways. No strings, no emotional bullshit. It's a business transaction. The girl walks away with a part of the proceeds, and everybody gets what they want."

"And this is legal?"

"Sure. It's gotta be. The whole thing's consensual. No one's getting forced to do anything. These girls *want* to sell their virginity."

Ben started. "They're virgins?"

"Not all of them, but if you want a virgin, you got to bid higher. I always bid high." He clinked glasses with Derek.

Ben lowered his eyelids to hide his emotions. "Why do you want to fuck around with virgins?"

"Because it's fun popping their cherries. Girls always remember their first time, and I live on in the memories of so many girls, I've lost count."

Ben helped himself to another shot to wash away the revolting image of Jake pounding away at some poor young woman. He looked Jake square in the eyes. "Not man enough to take on a woman of more experience?"

Though Ben's tone and following smile could have

been mistaken for a casual ribbing, Jake stiffened and frowned. He replied seriously, "Virgins are...cleaner. I like knowing that some other guy's gunk hasn't been inside her."

"But all the chicks at the Scarlet Auction have been tested, so you don't have to worry about disease and shit," Derek said. "You wouldn't know that, just getting to know a chick by dating. The Scarlet Auction makes sex much more...efficient."

Jason leaned in closer. "So whaddya say, Ben? You gonna come with tonight?"

CHAPTER TWO

With trembling hands, Kimani Taylor adjusted her simple black cocktail dress with spaghetti straps as she waited behind the stage where the auction was to be held. She closed her eyes and took in a deep breath.

I can't believe I'm doing this.

But she had made it this far, though at various points, she had thought to back out. There were the legal documents she'd had to sign with four different attorneys watching; the invasive questionnaire asking when she had lost her virginity and how many sexual partners she'd had in her life; the physical exam; and finally an interview with a woman asking about her sexual habits and preferences, such as whether or not she engaged in any hardcore BDSM.

"The more amenable you are, the more likely you will get bid on," the woman had told her.

"I guess you could say I'm open to it," Kimani had replied, reminding herself that her answers didn't ultimately matter. Her plan was to get bid on, get to know her "buyer" and the other participants of the Scarlet Auction, pull out before any sex actually happened, then write the scoop that would land her a job with the *San Francisco Tribune*.

"It's too risky for our paper to take on," the *Tribune's* editor, Sam Green, had told her. He had seemed very intrigued when she had first pitched the story but had since consulted the in-house attorney.

"But as a freelancer, I can," Kimani had replied. "I'll get the story and you can decide afterwards if it's worth printing."

"We could use an exposé. Our paper hasn't had anything like this before. If you can hit a homerun with your story, there'll be a job here for you."

Kimani had hardly been able to contain her glee at such an opportunity. Newspapers across the country were downsizing, and competition for reporting positions were at an all time high with many seasoned journalists having a hard time landing a job. Given she was only a year out of journalism school, she needed an edge, a scoop worthy of being noticed.

"No pressure, though," Sam had added. "If there should be an opening here, I will definitely give you a call. You were my favorite student in class."

"There weren't that many of us," she had said, referring to the course on the intersection of journalism and public policy that Sam had taught as a guest lecturer.

"Still, I could see you were talented. But going undercover can be dangerous. You know that, right? And you've never done anything like this before."

But Kimani didn't feel as if she had much of a choice. And it wasn't just about landing a job with a paper.

"I am *sooooo* excited," whispered a beautiful and petite blond standing next to her.

Kimani couldn't help but take in the young woman's boobs, which were practically spilling out of her pink skin-tight dress, and wonder if they were real since they were so large compared to the petite frame they were attached to.

"I'm *sooooo* ready to fall in love with a billionaire," she said, blue eyes sparkling.

Kimani cleared her throat, hardly able to believe her ears. "Does the Scarlet Auction have a matchmaking component?"

"No, but in all the books I read, the girl and billionaire always fall in love."

Kimani studied the blond and decided she couldn't be much older than eighteen or nineteen years old. Should she attempt to burst the young woman's bubble and warn her that the bidders weren't all going to Prince Charming?

No, she wasn't here to offer her own opinions. She was here to understand how the Scarlet Auction worked and to make connections with the subjects, which had not gone as she had wanted. The women had been isolated from one another until now, just as they were about to head on stage for the bidding. She would have to follow up with the other participants afterwards. Hopefully one or more would be willing to go on record with their experiences.

"They're not all billionaires," said a brunette

behind them.

"Close enough," replied the blond. "The Scarlet Auction doesn't just let any rich guy attend. He's got to have a net worth of at least nine figures, so you're not going to find ordinary millionaires."

"What's wrong with ordinary millionaires?" asked a slim woman with olive skin and long black hair. "A million dollars is probably more than I'll ever see in a lifetime."

There were just under two dozen women present, all between the ages of eighteen and thirty, beautiful and primped as if they were participating in a beauty pageant instead of an auction. Kimani herself had straightened her hair — which she usually didn't like to do because it was more effort than she had time for — and then used a curling iron at the ends. She needed to get selected or there would be no story. So she had traded her glasses for contacts and tried to make herself as appealing to as many men as possible.

"I heard a virgin at last month's auction got a bid of one hundred thousand dollars!" another woman said.

"That's why I've been saving myself for this moment," the blond said as she tugged at one of her long golden curls. "Virgins always get the higher bids."

"Did any of you get to finish reading the contract and nondisclosure agreement?" Kimani asked, recalling that she had been given only fifteen minutes to review over twenty pages of legalese in small type and dozens of footnotes.

"If the auction is being held in California, why is arbitration held in Florida?" Kimani had asked after reading one of the clauses in the contract.

"The parent company is located there," an attorney had responded coldly.

When the fifteen minutes were over and she had objected that she hadn't finished reading, she had been told if she didn't sign, she wouldn't get to participate. So she had signed, telling herself that, NDA or no NDA, and no matter how many intimidating lawyers they shoved in her face, she had a right to report abuse and assault.

"Why would I want to read a boring legal document?" the blond returned. "The lawyer covered all the important stuff."

"You're not worried?"

Kimani wanted to blurt out how her roommate, who had participated in the Scarlet Auction, had ended up covered in bruises.

"Showtime," announced an older woman. "Remember your stage assignments, ladies."

Kimani was assigned to stand stage left of the podium and noticed that the blond virgin was stage right. Kimani's roommate, Marissa, had explained that the virgins always stand stage right.

"Eww, these guys are so much older than I thought they would be," the brunette whispered to Kimani.

"Most billionaires are," Kimani whispered back. She made sure the broach with the hidden spy camera was secured to her choker.

"And not very attractive."

"The guy in the middle row is cute," said another woman.

Kimani scanned the crowd of mostly older white men and one lone woman in her forties to find the one dubbed "cute." She gathered her fellow participant was referring to the guy with wavy brown hair flanked by a shorter man with a receding hairline and a tan-skinned Asian. They sat a little too far back for the camera in her broach to capture their faces well, but maybe with some technical wizardry, an image specialist could enlarge the footage enough to be clear.

"We will begin the bidding with item number one," declared the woman at the podium.

Item? Kimani shook her head. This was so much worse than Marissa had described.

The people in the audience all had bid cards, which they held up when they wanted to meet the price announced by the auctioneer. The blond virgin was sold to the cute one for eighty-thousand dollars. The young woman looked ready to jump for joy.

We're being sold like livestock. Kimani shivered. *What's wrong with these people?*

The thin woman with long black hair was sold to the only Asian man in the audience, and the other friend of the cute one had purchased a redhead. Kimani was the last one to be bid on.

At first, no one raised their card. Kimani flushed a little. The lack of bids couldn't have been because of her appearance. She was young enough—twenty-five years old—and attractive, with her light mocha skin and naturally long eyelashes. She kept herself in shape through running every morning but still had curves in the right places. Maybe this crowd just wasn't into her type.

"Why don't we start the bidding at five thousand," said the auctioneer.

The lone woman in the audience raised her card.

"Ten thousand? Do I see ten thousand?" asked the auctioneer.

A card went up from a man who had already purchased the brunette. Kimani perked up at the idea that she wouldn't be alone.

"Fifteen thousand?"

The woman raised her card again.

"Twenty thousand? How about twenty thousand for this exotic beauty?"

Kimani stifled a gag. *Just think of the job*, she told herself. If written well, maybe the story would even be worthy of consideration for the Pulitzer.

"All right," Sam had relented when she declared she was doing the story one way or another. "I'll support you in any way I can—unofficially, of course. Who knows, maybe you could be the next Alex Dolan or Nellie Bly."

"Thirty thousand."

Kimani started and saw that the cute one was holding up his card.

"Thirty thousand. Do I have thirty-five?" asked the

auctioneer.

No one raised their cards.

"Thirty thousand going once…twice…and sold to gentleman number fourteen."

Kimani did a quick calculation in her head. The women got to keep forty percent of the bid at the end of the week, so that meant she could pocket twelve thousand dollars, provided she didn't violate the terms of the contract or NDA. That was pretty darn good money—equal to three months of work for Kimani. But even so, was it worth spending a week having sex with a stranger?

She didn't plan on having sex, though. She was here to get her story. She'd stick it out for as long as she could to get as much info as possible because Sam said the story would be worth infinitely more if she could get actual names, but they had agreed that if there was any danger to her person, she was to get out ASAP. As soon as the guy laid a finger on her, she'd explain she was chickening out and call it quits. The auction had made her put up two thousand dollars as a nonrefundable "processing fee," paid in cash, which Sam had fronted for her. But the loss of money would be more than made up for by the story.

At the end of the auction they were ushered backstage, where each woman was led away by a staff member.

"Can you believe it?" squealed the blond. "I just made forty thousand dollars!"

"You get to keep forty percent," Kimani reminded

her kindly.

"I know!"

"If the bid was eighty thousand, you get to keep thirty-two thousand."

"Oh. But that's still amazing! I just saved myself years of work!" She held out her hand. "I'm Claire, by the way."

Kimani shook her hand, wondering if Claire was her real name. It had fallen from her lips, there was a good chance it was. "Nice to meet you."

Claire waited expectantly.

"Oh, um, my name is…Montana," Kimani said.

"Ladies, your limo awaits," said a female staffer. "Follow me."

"A limo!" Claire grinned from ear to ear.

"Where are we going?" Kimani asked the staff member.

"That's up to your Master."

Kimani bristled at that last word. "But don't we get to go home first? I was going to change out of this dress—"

"Your week begins now."

"But—can I at least grab my bag?"

"I have your belongings here with me."

The woman ushered them to the back of the theater where a stretch limo awaited. Claire eagerly bounced inside. Kimani eyed the limo driver, who held the door open, wondering if this was someone she could trust to help if things went awry, but she couldn't tell. He didn't meet her gaze. Her pulse quickened as she wondered if she should step into the limo.

"Did the guy—" she began.

"You mean your Master?" the staff member supplied.

"Yes, did he mention where we're going?"

"That doesn't really matter, does it? Your contract says that's for him to decide."

Kimani hesitated. She didn't have enough story material yet. When she had discovered the bruises Marissa had tried to keep hidden a month ago, Marissa had refused to admit anything at first. Kimani had persisted, but though Marissa had finally relented and told Kimani the truth, she had refused to say anything on the record. No amount of badgering, cajoling or bribing from Kimani could change her mind because she was convinced she would have to repay the twenty thousand dollars she had made from her participation in the Scarlet Auction.

"I didn't go through that for nothing," Marissa had told Kimani angrily.

At that, Kimani had backed off. It was obvious Marissa was in a lot of pain and just wanted to move on with her life.

But Kimani couldn't let it go. It wasn't right. It wasn't right that a man could beat Marissa up like that and get away with it. After a few more days of failing to convince Marissa to speak up, Kimani had decided that if Marissa wouldn't come forth, she would find someone who would.

Taking a deep breath, she got in the limo.

CHAPTER THREE

You missed out, cuz," Jason said over the phone. "The women at the auction were dope. I got myself a little Thai hottie. We're heading up to Jake's cabin in the morning. You wanna ride with?"

Ben stared out the floor-to-ceiling windows overlooking the city from the bedroom of his penthouse in Pac Heights. "I'm not up to spending a week with Jake and Derek. I just spent a month overseeing the plans for our new luxury resort in Thailand and visiting our investments in Germany. I've got this political committee to set up for our uncle."

"Oh, right. What's he running for again?"

"Mayor of Oakland. I don't have the patience to dick around with Jake and Derek."

"But Jake signed some amazing ballers, and if your dad is serious about recruiting foreign talent for the Golden Phoenix, Jake's your best bet."

The Golden Phoenix basketball team was sponsored by the Lee Family Corporation, and Ben's father was intent on building the team into a contender for the Chinese Basketball Association title.

"And dicking around with them is fun."

"They're overgrown teenagers," Ben said. "You're a Lee. You don't have to hang out with dipshits like them."

"You're starting to sound like an old fart."

Ben groaned. He didn't want to have this conversation with Jason, who was almost six years younger and the closest thing to a brother to Ben.

"Come on," Jason urged. "It's going to be a fun week, and if you're tired from working, you need a vacay. If you don't have a girl, maybe Jake will lend you one of his."

"Jake has more than one?"

"Totally! I didn't know you could bid on more than one. If I had known that, I would have gotten a second one. There was this pretty hot Korean…"

Ben tried to ignore the tug at his groin. He needed a good fuck and had contemplated making a visit to the pretty blond who lived three floors below, but she reminded him a little too much of his mother, a German Russian his father had met on a diplomatic trip to Berlin.

And Ben, who liked to spend most of the year in San Francisco, didn't want complications with neighbors. He had that in common with Jake. Sometimes he just wanted a fuck for fuck's sake and nothing else.

Maybe he should have gone with them to the Scarlet Auction.

Jason made a final pitch. "Besides, I rarely get to see you anymore, so it'd be great to hang together."

Pinching the bridge of his nose, Ben recalled what his uncle, Jason's father, had said to him once:

"You are the eldest of the number one son," Uncle had said. "It is your duty to look after your siblings and cousins."

"I'll go," Ben decided, "but I'll get myself up to this cabin."

"Awesome! See you soon."

Ben hung up and threw himself on his bed. *Fuck.* A week with Tweedledee and Tweedledum.

Unzipping his pants, he pulled out his cock and tugged. It wasn't as good as pounding pussy, but it would have to do for now. Tomorrow morning, he'd call his security detail, Bataar, and arrange a sparring match. That would alleviate some of the pent-up energy and frustration. Fucking was more soothing, but like masturbating, sparring would have to do.

****

Kimani couldn't shake the queasy feeling building inside her as the limo headed north on US 101. Marissa hadn't mentioned being whisked away directly from the auction to her bidder's place of choice. She talked about being locked up in a nice house and submitting to sexual acts she wasn't comfortable with. Sex, and even BDSM sex, was part of the bargain, Marissa had explained, but there were no safe words, and even if there were, she doubted her 'Master' would have cared.

It had made Kimani sick to hear it. At first, Marissa had played off her injuries like they were nothing. If Kimani hadn't accidentally walked in on Marissa just as she was getting out of the shower, she would have never known about the bruises, which Marissa kept hidden beneath layers of clothes.

"They're just old bruises from the BDSM club I go to now and then," Marissa had said.

But when Kimani had pressed for details, Marissa's answers were increasingly suspicious.

"I bet Master has a mansion in Marin County," Claire prattled. "Or maybe he's meeting us at some fancy restaurant like The French Laundry."

Kimani would have loved the destination to be the famed Michelin-starred restaurant in Napa Valley, but she suspected that wasn't the case. She reached into her hobo handbag for her cell to text Sam what was happening.

"Hey! Where's my phone?"

She rifled through her purse, pulling out her glasses, ChapStick, notepad, and pens that had built-in audio recorders. Her canister of mace was missing, too.

Her heartbeat shot up. She turned to Claire, "Do you have your phone?"

Claire looked into her sparkling clutch. "Mine's missing, too. Oh, well, I don't really need it. I told my friends I was going away to a spa for some 'me' time."

Kimani tried not to panic. She tapped on the window separating her and the driver.

"Where is it we're going?" she asked as nonchalantly as possible to the driver.

"*No hablo ingles*," he replied.

Shit. Kimani willed herself to relax. Panicking wouldn't help her out. Sam knew where she was and what she was doing. If he didn't hear from her in some time, he'd get worried and do something.

Focus on getting the story.

"We are *soooooo* lucky," Claire cooed. "We got the hottest bidder. At first, I was really scared that the fat old guy in the front row was going to win me. I mean, I was *not* going to lose my virginity to that guy. I'd rather forfeit the two thousand dollars I put up, and getting that money wasn't easy. I'm still trying to pay off these girls."

Claire squeezed her boobs.

"Finally decided to take a cash advance on my credit card."

Kimani winced. The interest on that couldn't be pretty, but with over thirty thousand dollars coming her way, Claire shouldn't have trouble paying back the cash advance and the boob job.

"So what made you decide to do the Scarlet Auction?" Kimani asked as she settled in the leather upholstery across from Claire. She thought about clicking on one of her audio-recording pens, but she only had three of them with her and wanted to adhere to journalist ethics. She couldn't record without the source's permission unless lives were at stake, the information could not be obtained in any other way, or the story would suffer irrevocably without the information.

"Who wouldn't?" Claire responded. "How else can you make forty thousand in just one week? I mean, it's tons more than Julia Roberts made in *Pretty Woman*!"

"I don't know that—" Kimani stopped herself from suggesting that movies didn't necessarily make good examples for real life. "I bet lots of entrepreneurs can make that kind of money."

"I mean regular people, silly. It would take my older sister a whole year—maybe more—to make what I just did in one week!"

In a good mood, Claire chattered on about how being a barista like her sister or taking some other equally boring job was "*soooooo* not my thing." She talked about where she went to high school, how none of the classes at the local community colleges interested her, and that she had decided to go into modeling instead. But that career path was going slower than she would have liked as she worked more trade shows than she did photo shoots. She complained about the number of European women who came to the US to try their hand at modeling, and because foreigners were taking jobs away from Americans, she'd voted for Trump. She wanted to become a model and marry a billionaire like Melania.

"But maybe I'll get to marry a billionaire first," Claire said with a smile.

Kimani stared. Did Claire really think something

was going to come out of a relationship — if it could even be called that — with a guy who *paid* for sex?

"I'm actually a little nervous," Kimani said as she noticed that they were long past Marin County and driving through Sonoma County. "We don't know anything about this guy. What if he's not that nice?"

"Did you see how good-looking he was?"

Kimani did a double-take, not understanding the response.

"He had the sweetest-looking baby-blue eyes," Claire sighed. "And we know he's not racist 'cause, you know, he bid on you. That's a good sign, right?"

Kimani tapped on the window to the driver again. She wanted to get to a phone to call Sam with an update. "Can we make a bathroom stop?"

"*Lo siento, no hablo ingles,*" the driver replied.

Wishing she had paid more attention in her Spanish class, Kimani combed her memory and finally remembered. "*Baño, por favor.*"

"*Una hora.*"

"What did he say?" Claire asked.

"I think he said in an hour," Kimani replied. Where the hell where they being taken?

"I hope we get something to eat. Honestly, I thought the limo would be stocked with champagne or something. Instead, there's only bottled water."

At nearly four in the morning, they pulled into a refueling station somewhere north of Ukiah in Mendocino County. Kimani had never been this far north of San Francisco before. So much for dining at

The French Laundry.

After ducking out of view from the driver, Kimani found an old-fashioned pay phone. But it didn't work. The place was deserted with no trucks in sight, so she couldn't borrow a cell from anyone.

"*Chica! Vamanos!*" the driver called to her.

For a second, Kimani contemplated taking her chances with the empty truck stop, but her story wasn't complete.

"Coming," she called.

Claire napped while they continued their drive, but Kimani was too distracted to sleep. She told herself she was probably worrying about nothing. Not all the Scarlet Auction bidders were like Marissa's. Still, she wanted to remain vigilant and at least keep track of where they were. She kicked herself for not keeping her cell with her, but who would have thought it would get taken? Notice was probably on page nineteen of the contract in eight-point font.

Not long after leaving the truck stop, they pulled off US 101 and onto State Route 36. They passed towns Kimani had never heard of. All she knew was that they were likely in Trinity County, one of the least-populated counties in the state.

We're in the boonies.

Kimani hadn't noticed a single traffic light. It was doubtful the county even had a Starbucks. Getting off State Route 36, the limo drove along a heavily forested, winding road.

What if our guy is worse than Marissa's?

She tried to shake the morbid thoughts from her head, but every nerve in her body was screaming that she had gotten herself into a heap of trouble.

CHAPTER FOUR

"Holy shit," Claire gasped when the limo pulled up in front of a two-story cabin sitting at the edge of a small, pristine lake. "Now this is what I'm talking about."

Instead of awe, Kimani felt only dread. They were miles away from civilization, without their cellphones, with a driver who didn't speak English.

"I don't understand why, if we were coming this far, we didn't get to pack bags?" Kimani wondered, clutching her handbag close to her. She wanted to be able to switch on one of her recording pens when needed.

"Probably because we have a closetful of fancy clothes just waiting for us!" Claire replied, clasping her hands together.

Kimani raised her eyebrows. "I've got a bad feeling about this. Seriously, we have no idea where we are, who we're dealing with…"

That truck stop back in Mendocino County was looking like it would have been the wiser choice.

"You don't get it," Claire responded. "We're *his* for a week. We're here because he wants us all to himself with no distractions. We can't get away, and we're totally at his mercy. It's *sooooo* sexy!"

"Seriously, you don't find this creepy at all?"

Claire shook her head and followed the limo driver up the stone walkway to the cabin. Kimani took a bracing breath and trailed behind. Maybe she was overreacting. Maybe the guy was just planning a romantic weekend at his cabin. His remote cabin.

"Oh! This is probably where we meet the kind old housekeeper or personal assistant that helps Master out with everything and helps us get dressed," Claire said to Kimani. "She likes that he has a woman in his life."

Kimani stared in disbelief. Did Claire really think reality was going to unfold like some erotic romance story? Still too unsettled to appreciate the beautiful natural surroundings, Kimani focused on the cabin. At any other time, it would have taken her breath away with its seven gables, multiple balconies, and windows that took up ninety percent of the cabin's facade. The place probably raked in a huge heating bill in winter. Kimani felt some relief to see that with all the balconies, there were many points of egress.

A stern-looking man opened the double doors of oak and decorative glass with satin-nickel caming. With his height and bulk, the guy did not look like someone to mess with.

"*Las chicas*," the driver said.

Mr. Stern-Face nodded. "This way, ladies."

Kimani decided she preferred the company of the non-English speaking driver, but the man was headed back to the limo. She and Claire followed Stern-Face into the cabin and downstairs to what was a third but lower level of the cabin. He opened the door to a large single room.

"This is where you'll sleep."

Claire walked in, ready to be impressed. Instead, her face fell. There was no beautiful four-post bed draped in romantic linen, no plush carpeting or shiny hardwood floors, no door to an amazing bathroom with granite counters and a Jacuzzi bathtub. There were no windows, and the only light came from a lightbulb at the top of the ceiling. The only furnishing comprised two queen-size mattresses resting directly on the floor without box springs.

"You're to stay in the room until he gets here," Stern-Face said before shutting the door behind him.

"Wait!" Kimani cried. She ran to the door but found it locked. Shit. She went to the only other door, but it only led to a toilet.

"This is not what I expected at all," Claire said. "It must be like some kind of joke. Maybe we'll be shown our real rooms after we go shopping."

"I don't think there's much in the way of luxury shopping in this county," Kimani murmured as she went to try the door again. No luck. "I can't believe we're locked in here!"

"Master doesn't want us escaping," Claire giggled.

Kimani stayed the desire to smack some sense into the girl.

"I wish we had something to eat, though. I'm

starving."

Kimani dug into the purse she still held and fished out a packet of trail mix, which she offered to Claire. She didn't have much of an appetite.

Claire hopped off the bed. "Oh, thanks! I'll just have a little since we're probably going to have a sinfully decadent breakfast."

"You sure about that?"

"Billionaires like to wine and dine in style. I mean, what's the point of being a billionaire if you don't indulge in everything that you can?"

"I don't know about that. Gold toilets would be excessive to me."

Claire shrugged. "If you've got money to burn, why not?"

Kimani didn't answer. Her mind was on more pressing considerations, like how to escape if the situation warranted it. Maybe this was part of the fantasy — it obviously was for Claire — and when the week was over, they'd laugh and talk about how fun it was.

But this guy expected sex, and when Kimani refused, what would happen? Would he be understanding and have his limo take her back to the city? Or would he be a jerk and dump her at the nearest town to fend for herself?

Or what if he didn't take "no" for an answer?

Since he hadn't received an update in a while, Sam would probably be worried by now. His cell was connected to hers through a locater app. He could trace where her phone was—unless whoever had it turned the device off or it ran out of battery.

Remember the story. It's going to be killer. It's going to be worth it.

Feeling better, Kimani took a reassuring breath. She sat down on the bed. Wow. The sheets were amazing. She had never felt anything so soft.

The sound of footsteps made her jump to her feet. Was it Stern-Face? Could she get him to let her use a phone?

The door opened, and in walked their bidder. Their *Master.*

CHAPTER FIVE

T he guy had boyish good looks with wavy golden-brown hair and twinkling blue eyes. He reminded Kimani of a young Bradley Cooper. So with looks like his, why did he need to buy women at the Scarlet Auction, she wondered?

He put his hands on his hips. In his Kiton jeans and perfectly pressed shirt by Tom Ford, he looked impeccable — the opposite of how Kimani felt.

Claire waved. "Hi, I'm Claire."

He frowned. "I didn't say you could talk."

"Oh! Sorry! I mean..." Claire looked down.

"And I don't know any Claire. Your name's Slut #1." He turned to Kimani. "And you're Slut #2."

Kimani felt her cheeks burn.

"Let's get a couple things straight here," he continued. "You don't talk unless I say you can. You don't do *anything* — and that includes taking a piss — without my permission. Got it?"

Claire nodded. He turned his gaze onto Kimani, waiting. She stared at him, wondering if he was serious or just acting out a role?

The next second, her cheek was on fire and pain flared in her temple from where her head struck

Claire's.

"Answer me, bitch!"

She had to blink several times to get her bearing.

"Well?" he demanded.

Surely the Silent Auction arrangement didn't allow for violence? Even if the contract she signed acknowledged she might be, in BDSM parlance, 'disciplined,' assault couldn't stand up in court, could it? But she decided not to risk the guy's ire and answered, "Yeah, I got it."

He struck her again. This time Claire jumped out of the way.

"I didn't say you could talk, bitch."

This shit just got real, Kimani realized. Her heart was racing. Part of her was recalling all the moves she had learned in her self-defense class. The other part reminded her what she was here for. She wished she had turned on the broach camera or had her recording pen ready.

She heard him unbuckle his belt.

"Now how about some breakfast?"

Turning, she saw that he had taken out his cock. *Shit.*

"Come on, slave," he said to Claire, waving his penis up and down. "Time to eat."

For the first time since the auction, Claire looked uncertain.

"Don't make me say it twice," he threatened.

Tentatively, Claire went down on her knees before him.

"What's the matter? Never done a blow job before?"

Claire shook her head.

He smiled. "Well, you're in for a treat. Go on now. Take that puppy into your mouth."

He pointed his cock at her. Claire parted her lips.

"Oh, that's good," he groaned as he slid into her mouth.

His hand went to the back of her head as he began thrusting his hips. She grunted as he tried to shove more of his length into her.

"Yeah, baby," he said. "Good slaves get rewarded. Bad slaves get punished."

Claire choked when he shoved a little too hard.

"All right, all right," he said when she began gagging uncontrollably. He turned to Kimani. "Your turn."

"I'm not ready yet," she said.

He narrowed his eyes. "What did I say about talking?"

"Aren't there supposed to be safe words?" she blurted, as a new worry blossomed. What if they were dealing with a psychopath?

He shook his head. "Are all niggers as dumb as you?"

Her ears burned at the epithet. There was no way she was taking this asshole's cock now. For a brief moment, she had contemplated doing it for the sake of the story. Not anymore. Now she was as much pissed as she was scared.

"You just lost your privilege to wear clothes," he declared. "Take the dress off. Now."

Every nerve in her body revolted at the command, but when she didn't move, he took a step toward her and struck her across the cheek, this time with his fist. Claire screamed.

"I told you to take the fucking dress off!"

Tears pressed into Kimani's eyes as she unzipped the dress with shaky hands. The situation shouldn't have surprised her. She had fully expected to find her owner to be no different than the man who had abused Marissa, had known there was a chance she would get physically hurt. Unlike Marissa, she wouldn't just sit around and take it.

However, she hadn't anticipated being without her cellphone. She hadn't anticipated being so far from civilization with nowhere to run. Now if she put up resistance, there was no one she could turn to and no escape. How violent would this guy get? Was he going to beat her until she took his cock?

But he had gone back to Claire. He took her jaw and opened her mouth before sliding himself in.

"You sure look pretty eating cock," he cooed to her before looking up to see if Kimani was still undressing.

With the zipper down, she slid the straps from her shoulders.

"Take it all off, bitch."

Trembling the whole time, she pushed the dress past her hips and down her legs.

"Bra and panties, too."

Reaching behind her, she unclasped her bra. Why hadn't she thought to hide a weapon of some sort in her dress? Should she try to make a run for it and escape to tell the authorities? Her own experience could serve as the basis for the story. But was that enough?

She hesitated at her boy-cut briefs and expected the asshole to bark at her again, but he was too distracted by his blow job. He was moaning and babbling incoherently as he fucked Claire in the face. Soon he was blowing his load all over her.

"Took care of one virginity," he chuckled as he tugged at his semi-flaccid cock.

He glanced at Kimani. She quickly shed her panties. Except for her heels, she was now completely naked.

"Now about you—" he began before he was interrupted by the ringing of his cellphone. Cradling the phone between his ear and shoulder, he put his penis back in his pants and zipped up. "Hold on. I don't have good reception downstairs. Give me a minute."

He took his cellphone in hand and walked out the door, closing it behind him. The lock turned.

"You okay?" Kimani asked Claire, who was still on her knees, wiping the cum off her face with her hands. She went into the bathroom and got some tissue for Claire.

"Y-Yeah," Claire answered. "It—It was different from what I expected. He's really into an alpha dominant role."

Kimani couldn't believe it. "The only role that guy is into is the role of asshole."

She rubbed where he had punched her. She had known from Marissa's experience that things could turn violent, but she hadn't been prepared enough. The wisest course of action was to find a way to get herself and Claire the hell out. Who knew what else this asshole was capable of?

But how could they escape? Where would they go? And even if they could, what recourse did they have? She didn't know a thing about the guy. The best she could provide the police would be a sketch of what he looked like. The guy deserved to be arrested for assault, maybe even kidnapping.

His attorneys, as well as those for the Scarlet Auction, would probably make conviction a challenge. They might even try to explain his behavior away like Claire did. There was a misunderstanding, he thought he was just acting out the part of a Master-Slave relationship in the context of consensual BDSM, he thought he was just doing what the women wanted, etc.

And who knew what she and the other women had agreed to in signing those legal forms.

Kimani bit her lower lip. If she wanted to see this son of a bitch put away, she needed more evidence. But how was she going to get it?

CHAPTER SIX

Ben didn't bother changing out of his dark colored suit and indigo dress shirt. His morning meetings had run longer than anticipated, and he didn't want to arrive much later than Jason would. He needed to be there to make sure his cousin didn't do anything stupid with Jake and Derek.

Ben's jet landed at Weaverville Airport, where his rental was waiting for him. After putting his bags in the Jeep rental, he drove himself to the cabin. With its rugged landscape of heavy forestry and the Klamath Mountains, the area was beautiful. Unlike most years, the terrain was verdant with flora as a result of the heavier-than-usual rain in the spring months. Ben had put down the top of the Jeep to bask in the early summer sun, glad to be in dry and temperate Northern California instead of muggy and hot Beijing, where his parents lived.

At the cabin, a stocky man named Vince opened the door. At 6'2", Ben stood taller than most of his friends, save for the ones playing in the CBA, but Vince was easily a head taller than Ben. He didn't know why, but the first thought Ben had on meeting Vince was whether or not he could take the guy out. He was confident he could. Men with Vince's build tended to be slower and less agile.

Jake appeared in the foyer. "Benji, glad you could make it."

The hairs on Ben's neck curled. Had Jake just called him *Benji*?

"Only my mom and sisters ever call me Benji."

"Oh, hey, no problem, brah."

"Where's Jason?"

"He and Derek are coming up together, and their driver got lost. You like bourbon? I was about to open up a bottle of Kentucky straight. It's uncut and unfiltered."

Vince offered to take Ben's bags up to his room, the last one on the left upstairs, so Ben followed Jake into the great room with floor-to-ceiling windows that looked out onto the lake. Jake walked over to the bar, but Ben stopped at the threshold.

At the left end of the room before the fireplace knelt two women. One was a blond in a tight pink faux leather dress. The other was completely naked. Both of them looked disheveled.

"What the fuck?" Ben let drop.

"I see you found my acquisitions," Jake drawled as he opened the bottle of whiskey.

Ben met the eyes of the blond. She glanced down as if not wanting to be caught looking. The other woman stared at him with what seemed like defiance and suspicion. His gaze did a quick sweep of her figure, and his groin tightened of its own accord. She had nice B-cup breasts with dark chocolate areolas, a smooth stomach that led to swollen hips and a cute patch of curls between shapely thighs.

Her left cheek appeared a little discolored and swollen. Her hair was partially and unevenly straightened, and her mascara had spread below her eyes as if she had slept without taking her makeup off.

Jake handed him a glass of bourbon. "You missed out, man. There were prime pickings last night."

Ben glanced at the women again. For women who wanted this shit, they didn't look too happy at the moment.

"Do you have the portfolios I requested?" Ben asked Jake.

"Yeah, but you really want to talk business right now? You just got here."

"Now's as good a time as any. Better. We don't have to bore Jason and Derek."

"Fine, fine."

Jake went to sit at a table before the window. He gestured to the manila folders. "They're all right here. You'll want this guy, though. Jamaal Dixon. He's playing in the EuroLeague right now."

Ben set his bourbon down on the table and leafed through the portfolios. When transacting business, he preferred not to drink. It was hard enough keeping his mind on business with two women, one of them naked, kneeling just yards from where he sat.

"They just going to kneel there the whole time?" he asked, trying to keep his gaze off the naked one — especially her tits and pelvis.

"That's what slaves do," Jake replied as he poured himself more bourbon. "Whatever I tell them to do."

"Why is one of them naked?"

"Oh, that was her preference."

From the corner of his eye, he saw the young woman stiffen.

"What about the one from UCLA?" Ben asked. "Coach saw him at an exhibition game and likes the way he plays."

"You'll have to pay good money for Tyrell Jenkins. He could have been a second-round draft pick if he didn't have that sprain late last year."

They talked about the merits of the different players and the salary each was likely to command. The discussion went slowly because Jake had had three shots and wasn't too focused on business.

"Give Tyrell a call," Ben said.

"I don't know that he'd consider going off to live in China."

"Have you asked him?"

"No."

"Then feel him out."

"Okay, I'll feel him out."

Ben waited.

Jake stared back. "What? Now?"

"Now."

Jake's whole body seemed to curl. "Fine. Since you

sound like you're in a hurry, Benji."

Ben gave him a hard look. "Only people with pussies call me Benji. You got a pussy, Jake?"

"Chill. I just forgot."

After Jake pulled out his cellphone and wandered back to the bar to add ice to his glass, Ben sauntered over to the women. The blond looked really young. Like she was barely legal.

"How long have you been kneeling here?" he inquired.

The blond didn't answer and continued to stare at the rug that probably didn't provide much cushioning from the shiny hardwood floor. The other woman glanced over to Jake before answering, "Three hours."

Three hours. Jake was a bigger asshole than he'd thought. Ben played around with heavy BDSM, but he had never made a woman kneel for three hours straight.

"You got a name?"

Again, the blond remained silent.

"Apparently, we're Slut #1 and Slut #2," replied the naked one.

She said it as if it was his fault she had a name she obviously didn't like. She didn't like him, either. Ben sensed that right away. A porcupine was less prickly than her.

"Tyrell didn't pick up, but I left him a message," Jake said as he walked over with his shot glass refilled. "No use talking to my slaves. They're not supposed to talk without my say so."

Ben raised his brows. "And they signed up for this?"

Jake rolled his eyes. "They're getting compensated a shitload of money for their time. Plus, they get to live out their *Fifty Shades of Grey* fantasies."

"How much do they get?"

"I don't know exactly. I paid just over a hundred thousand for blondie and the black girl."

The blond's stomach growled.

"Are you hungry?" Ben asked.

Jake grabbed his crotch. "I fed her this morning."

The prospect of food made the blond look up.

"If they've been kneeling here for three hours, they're probably hungry. Don't you feed your slaves?"

"Sure. I just—it wasn't lunchtime yet."

Ben looked at his watch. "It's past noon. Get them something to eat."

Jake stared at him in disbelief. Ben could tell he wasn't making any friends ordering Jake about, but he wasn't interested in being the guy's *brah*.

"You *are* the host," Ben added.

With a discontented snort, Jake walked over to the expansive Tuscan-inspired kitchen, opened up the well-stocked refrigerator and pulled out a brand-new jar of pickles. Walking back, he set the jar on the coffee table near the women.

Ben crossed his arms. "Open it."

"They're not incompetent." Jake nodded to the blond. "Help yourself to some pickles, slut."

The blond reached for the jar and tried to twist the

cap off. Jake had already stalked off to the bar, so Ben took the jar from the blond and twisted the cap off for her. She reached in eagerly for a pickle.

"Just Slut #1," Jake called from the bar. "I'm not happy with the other one."

Ben looked at the second woman, expecting her to hang her head in disappointment. Her stomach had rumbled, too. Instead, she seemed to expect Jake's response. Her jaw tightened and her eyes flashed.

"How come?" Ben inquired.

"She wouldn't eat her breakfast." Jake smiled as if listening to some silent inside joke.

Ben looked at her cheek again. Though her skin was darker than what Ben was used to assessing, the discoloration in her cheek was definitely the beginning of a bruise. "So you hit her?"

"I didn't hit her. What do you mean?"

"Her cheek." *Dipshit.*

"What about her cheek?"

"It looks swollen."

Jake shrugged his shoulders. "I didn't notice anything. I'm gonna go see if Vince went to pick up some lunch."

After Jake had left and while the blond was finishing off her third pickle, Ben turned to the older woman. She looked to be in her mid-twenties. She also looked intelligent. He had noticed her studying him, sizing him up. He sensed she was a little on edge but didn't want to show it. Only when his gaze dropped to her naked body—he couldn't help but look at those inviting curves—did she show any discomfort. When his gaze went back to her eyes, he read their message loud and clear.

Fuck you, they said.

"Just got a text from Derek that they're almost here," Jake announced upon returning.

"How much for her?" Ben asked. The words were out of his mouth before he could think on them.

"What's that?"

"How much? I want to buy her."

CHAPTER SEVEN

Kimani blinked in disbelief. She wasn't sure if she should be glad or not that the tall guy who didn't like to be called Benji wanted her. If it had been a different place, a different situation, she would have found the guy hella good-looking with his wide brow, piercing black eyes, and strong jawline. But since he was a friend or associate of Master Asshole, she wasn't about to give him credit for anything.

"She's not for sale," replied Jake.

She had heard him introduce himself on the call to Tyrell. Now that she had a first name and knew that he was involved in the sports profession, she could probably figure out who he really was. But she didn't just want to embarrass him by writing an expose. Even with the #MeToo movement happening, a guy like him would probably just get off with a slap on the hand.

"You had your chance," Jake continued. "You chose not to go to the auction."

"I'll pay double. Take her off your hands."

"I can handle two."

Benji didn't say anything, but Kimani sensed he questioned Jake's ability.

"Besides, I want to see what jungle fever is all about," Jake drawled. "I've never fucked black pussy before."

"Two hundred thousand."

Kimani felt her eyes pop out of her head. How did these people throw money around like this? There were hard-working people who would never come close to having that kind of money to spend on frivolous things like a week with a sex slave.

"Be a good host," Benji coaxed as if talking to a child. "Give me the girl for two hundred thousand."

Jake narrowed his eyes. "Why you want her so bad?"

"Why do you? Sounds like she's not a well-behaved slut."

"She just needs some disciplining."

"I can handle that. Two hundred is my last offer."

Jake pursed his lips and scratched his chin. "Fine. You can have her. Even though it was your choice to come stag, I'd feel bad if you didn't have any pussy like the rest of us. Have the money wired to my account."

A long silence ensued.

"Fuck lunch," Jake said at last. "I'm going on the boat. You wanna go on the boat, Slut #1?"

Claire gave a timid nod. Grabbing her hand, he stomped off with her, leaving Kimani alone with Benji.

Her pulse quickened as they stared at one another. As much of an asshole as Jake was, was this man the lesser evil? She was comforted a little by the fact Benji was nice enough to request food on their behalf, and as she found herself pulled into the ebony pools of his eyes, an odd and kindred sensation wound around her heart. Maybe it was their shared dislike of Jake.

The man was taller than most Asians she knew, and when he removed his jacket and rolled up his shirtsleeves, her breath faltered. He had looked model-perfect in his suit, but with his jacket off, she could see he had a really nice build.

His gaze traveled her body, taking in every naked inch. She flushed beneath his study. She had convinced herself not to care about being undressed before Jake. The asshole was deliberately trying to make her feel exposed, vulnerable and degraded. She wasn't going to give him the satisfaction. But with the current pair of intense, clear eyes staring at her, she felt self-conscious.

Her stomach grumbled, and she glanced at the pickle jar. Normally she wasn't a fan of pickles, but she was pretty hungry at the moment.

Seeing the focus of her gaze, he said, "Go on, have some."

She reached into the jar and pulled out a slice but kept him in her line of sight in case he made any sudden movement.

After laying his jacket over the back of the sofa, he walked over to the kitchen. She watched him assemble a bag of ice, which he brought to her.

"For your cheek," he explained.

Finishing the pickle slice, she accepted the ice and

pressed it to her face.

"Thank you…" He hadn't said how she should address him, so she used what the Scarlet Auction staff had recommended. "Master."

"Where'd you get the bruise?"

She didn't respond. She was pretty sure he and Jake weren't the best of friends, but she didn't want to assume too much. What if he told Jake? What if Jake called off the deal and punished her for contravening what he had said? She had already decided she was going to gather as much evidence as possible so that she could nail Jake's ass to the wall.

When she didn't answer, Benji didn't press. Instead, he went back to the kitchen and made tea using some fancy coffee machine. He brought over two steaming mugs.

"I'm not much of a tea drinker," she said.

"Drink it anyway."

Setting down the ice, she took the mug he held out for her. Ugh. Green tea. Her least favorite.

"Sit down," he said as he took a seat on the sofa opposite her.

Sitting down had never felt so good. She had taken to shifting her weight from one side to the other to provide some relief for her poor aching knees.

"On the sofa," he added when she plopped down on the floor.

She crawled onto the sofa and pulled up her knees to provide some coverage for her nakedness.

"What's your name?" he asked after taking a sip of

his tea.

She didn't see many guys his age drink tea, especially when there was expensive alcohol around as an option. She noticed he had barely touched his bourbon. Jake had also mentioned he'd opted out of the Scarlet Auction. Why was that?

"Your real name," he clarified.

Did that mean he wasn't going to call her Slut #2?

"Montana."

He raised his brows. "Don't know many black women named Montana."

She almost retorted that she doubted he knew many black people at all. To keep herself from saying anything, she sipped her tea and grimaced at the flavor. For a spell, he did nothing but drink his tea and watch her.

"There any coffee?" she ventured to ask finally, hoping to make him go into the kitchen.

"Tea's better for you."

Patronizing bastard. His gaze was at her tits. Looking away, he shifted on the sofa and cleared his throat.

"You mind if I get dressed?" she decided to ask, hoping that he wasn't as big an asshole as Jake. "It's a little cold in here."

He deliberated for a moment before answering, "I'd prefer you didn't."

She clenched her jaw in disappointment. So much for him being the nice guy. When she met his gaze, she had the strange feeling he was testing her.

"You went to Nerd Nation," he commented, eying her class ring.

She looked at him, startled. Most people didn't know Stanford by that moniker.

"I was there, too," he added. "For my MBA."

That doesn't mean we have anything in common she wanted to say. The people in the graduate school of business were a world apart from the activists and liberal arts undergraduates she'd hung out with.

"What did you study?" he asked.

"Communications."

"No wonder you need money."

She sucked in her breath, wanting to tell him she *didn't* need the money, especially his. Well, not that she couldn't use more — a lot more — to pay off her student loans, but it wasn't like she was destitute. Especially not after she got hired at the *Tribune.*

"How much do you get from the Scarlet Auction?" he asked next.

"Forty percent."

Out of two hundred thousand, that would be eighty thousand dollars. She could do a lot with eighty thousand dollars. But his transaction was directly with Jake, so she wouldn't see any of it.

Vince walked in carrying bags of what was probably lunch. He leered at her as he walked by before placing the bags on the table.

"Where's Jake?" Vince asked.

"On the water," Benji replied.

Vince helped himself to some bourbon, then sat

down at the table and unpacked a sandwich for himself. Benji's cellphone rang and Kimani heard a guy on the line say, "Hey, Ben."

So his name was Ben. Might even be short for Benjamin. She stored the information in her mind to look up a guy named Ben or Benjamin that was associated with the Chinese Basketball Association and went to Stanford's business school. She was pretty sure she could come up with his full identity.

She couldn't make out everything the man calling Ben said, but she heard something about his date having a cousin willing to come to the lake.

"Don't bother. I got my own," Ben replied.

"Yeah? Cool," said the other guy "I mean, I'd share mine if I had to, but I'm not really into the threesome thing — unless it's two girls on one of me, of course. See you soon."

Kimani stayed the impulse to toss her tea at Vince, who blatantly ogled her as he chomped on his potato chips. Ben hung up his cell, glanced at Vince, then removed his jacket from the back of the sofa.

Rising to his feet, he held out his jacket to her. "You said you were cold."

She looked up at him first in surprise, then gratitude. Taking the jacket, she quickly shrugged it on. The material was *amazing*. She had never worn anything so silken before.

"What's here?" he asked Vince, peering into the bags on the table.

"Tri-tip, pulled pork and turkey," Vince answered.

Finishing, he wiped his crumbs off the table, threw the wrapper and potato chip bag in the wastebasket, and went off to do whatever it was he did. Before leaving, he spared Kimani only a brief glance, less interested now that she was covered.

"What's your preference?" Ben asked her.

"Um, turkey," she answered. He was being nice to her, but at some point, he was probably going to want a blow job just like Jake. Could she bring herself to do it for the sake of a story?

"Chips or potato salad?"

She shook her head. She hoped Claire was getting something better to eat than pickles, but she rather doubted it. They ate in silence at first, but she had too many questions to keep quiet. She wanted to know him better, for the story and so she could prepare herself for what might come.

"Can I ask a question?" she ventured.

"I don't have anything against you talking," he replied.

"Why weren't you at the Scarlet Auction last night?"

He propped his feet over the edge of the coffee table. "Why do you care?"

She shrugged her shoulders in feigned nonchalance. "Just making conversation. Jake only paid thirty thousand for me."

"Yeah?"

He sounded disinterested. She found herself unexpectedly staring at his mouth when he brushed away a dab of mayonnaise. He had sensuous lips. Almost as full as a brother's.

He turned the question on her. "What made you decide to do the Scarlet Auction? You that hard up for money?"

She was taken aback. Because Jake had shown no interest in learning about the women he had purchased, she had expected the same from Ben.

"Why do you care?" she threw back at him.

He stared at her, his eyes ever appraising. "Just making conversation."

She was irritated and amused all at once. "Sure, the money's good. Pretty damn good if you break it down to a per-hour wage."

"You don't have a problem prostituting yourself?"

She bristled. Was he trying to make a moral judgment? *He* was the one shelling out a ridiculous amount of money.

"If men don't have a problem paying for sex, why should women have a problem selling it?" she returned.

"They shouldn't. Your body, your choice."

She was stunned. He made prostitution sound like a progressive value. He wadded up the sandwich wrapper and tossed it into the wastebasket like he was making a jump shot. From the soft flick of his wrist, she could tell he had some shooting skills.

"You play," she commented.

"Do you?"

"In high school. I wasn't good enough to play for

Tara, however."

"Very few people are."

She couldn't help but like that he knew a little about Stanford women's basketball and the name of the coach. Most men knew next to nothing about women's team sports. Having eaten half her sandwich, she wrapped the other half to save for Claire.

"You ever watch the team play?" she asked.

"I took my younger sister to a few games. She thought about playing for VanDerveer."

"What position?"

"Small forward."

"That's the position I played — in high school. Did your sister go to Stanford?"

"UCLA."

"She must be really good."

"She is."

Kimani looked down. This was surreal. She was having a conversation about basketball while half-naked in a remote cabin with a stranger who had paid two hundred thousand dollars for sex without batting an eye.

He paid to own you for a week, she reminded herself, and reasoned that she was getting chummy with him so that she could learn more for her story.

"You look like you could use a nap."

Her gaze snapped up. Was "nap" a code word for some kind of kinky sex?

"What's the matter?" he asked.

"Nothing. I…"

"You look tired."

Even if nap didn't mean anything else, she wasn't sure she wanted to go back down into that depressing basement.

"Go wash up and rest," he said. "I've got calls to make."

At her hesitation, he asked again, "What?"

"Wash up where?"

He gave her a puzzled look. "The bathroom."

"I don't think there's a sink in the basement."

He narrowed his eyes. "The basement? Show me."

Taking the sandwich, she got off the sofa and headed toward the staircase that would lead to the room she shared with Claire. Ben followed behind. She opened the door to the room and went to put the sandwich in her handbag. Ben looked around the room with a frown.

"Come with me. You can use my room. Grab your stuff."

She scooped up her bag and clothing.

"That's it? You don't have a suitcase or anything?"

"We came straight here from the auction."

He let out a long breath but only motioned for her to follow him.

Ben's room was the antithesis of the basement, with more floor-to-ceiling windows looking out over the lake and sliding glass doors that led to the balcony, a leather settee and chaise before a fireplace, and a gorgeous mahogany, king-size, four-post bed. This was the opulence that Claire was expecting.

Ben opened his suitcase and pulled out a white t-shirt and sweats, which he tossed to her.

"You can have those for now," he said. "The bathroom's over there."

Leaving the room, he closed the bedroom door behind him.

Alone, Kimani breathed in her first deep breath since arriving. The room was better than the basement. Ben was better than Jake. But she couldn't relax completely. There was an edge to Ben, and a temper could easily lie behind his cool exterior. But so far, it seemed that things were looking up for her.

The bathroom was equally as luxurious as the bedroom with its granite counters, porcelain-tiled flooring, shower with stone tiles, and a Jacuzzi bathtub. Seeing her reflection in the mirror, Kimani was surprised at how bad she looked. There was a definite bruise on her cheek, and her hair couldn't look worse.

Why had Ben paid two hundred thousand dollars for her? Because he hadn't brought a sex partner of his own?

After taking one of the longest showers of her life, she pulled on his t-shirt.

"Oh my God," she whispered at the softness of the fabric.

Passing by the bedroom door, she checked to see if it was locked. It opened. Unlike the basement door, she could lock this one from the inside. Should she lock it? Well, it would be safer if she was really going to take a nap. She didn't want to let down her guard in a cabin full of strangers, but she needed rest if she was going to be on her toes.

After locking the door, she drew the blinds and crawled into the bed. When she closed her eyes, she kept seeing Ben. At some point, he was going to want sex. There wasn't any other reason he would have paid a crapload of money for her. The question she had to decide was: how far was she willing to go for her story?

CHAPTER EIGHT

She had locked the bedroom door, so Ben couldn't get in the room to change, but he didn't let it bother him. It was probably better he had some distance from her. She had looked way too hot in his jacket, and his hands kept itching to slide under it and feel her up. Even with her stale makeup, she was pretty with those large brown eyes, thick lashes, and high cheekbones. But there was something else that drew him to her. Maybe it was the way her look shot daggers at Jake. Or maybe it was the defiant flare in her eyes.

Offering to buy her from Jake had not been in Ben's plan. He had been prepared to suck it up and be the odd wheel with no date. But she—Slut #2, Montana, or whatever her name was—had changed everything.

He had to have her. Or, he didn't want Jake to have her. Ben was pretty sure Jake had given her the bruise.

But now that she was *his*, what was he going to do with her?

Supposedly, she had signed up for a week of sex with a stranger. The logical thing would be to have sex with her, but he could tell she wasn't comfortable with her surroundings yet. And something was off. He couldn't tell what or why.

Heading back downstairs, he found that Jake

hadn't yet returned, so he made the calls he needed to make, including one to his uncle Gordon Lee, who was in a tight race for mayor of Oakland. Just as Ben finished up his third call, he heard the voices of men and women. Vince must have opened the door because seconds later, Derek and Jason spilled into the room. They must have been drinking on the ride up because they appeared off balance. Two giggling women followed behind them.

"Cuz, you beat us," said Jason.

"I took the jet," Ben replied.

"Ohhh, you have a jet?" the woman of Southeast Asian descent asked, stumbling toward him. She was as thin as a reed — maybe thinner. "Like a corporate jet or a private jet?"

"Ben has both, I'm sure, probably more," slurred Derek. "The Lees are one of the wealthiest families in China. What did *Forbes* peg you at? Twelve, thirteen billion?"

The eyes of the women lit up.

"That's impressive," said a redhead with a champagne glass in hand.

Jason wrapped an arm around his petite date. "Ben, this is Lisa. Pretty sweet find, hunh?"

The redhead introduced herself. "And I'm Ryan."

Jake returned then with the blond, who looked a little worse, as if she had been crying. She looked embarrassed to be wearing her pink cocktail dress while Lisa was casually dressed in a sundress and Ryan was in tight cropped leggings and a halter.

"Hi, I remember you," said Lisa to the blond. "You're Claire. You got the highest bid at the auction last night. Congratulations."

"There's no Claire here. Her name's Slut #1," Jake corrected.

The women did a double take, then Ryan turned to Derek. "Do I get a nickname, too?"

"Sure, you can be Slut #2," Derek replied.

Ryan giggled.

"That one's taken already," Jake informed

"Slut #3 it is."

"And that would make me Slut #4?" Lisa asked.

"She can count." Jake grinned at Jason.

"Of course she can. Asians are supposed to be good at math," Derek joked.

"Just select Asians: Chinese, Korean, Japanese and Indian," Jason said.

"Are you saying I'm not as smart because I'm Thai?" Lisa demanded.

Jason pulled her to him and kissed her neck. "Pretty much, babe."

"I did hate math. It was so boring, but I got a passing grade because all the boys around me would do the work for me. I call that being smart."

"Here, you're graded on something much more fun than math."

They touched foreheads, and Lisa giggled.

Ben turned to Claire. "There are sandwiches on the table."

She glanced timidly at Jake, as if not daring to hope

for the chance to eat. Ben decided he would have to beat the motherfucker up if he didn't feed her.

Jake had walked over to the table. To Claire, he said, "Go over to your spot. Be good and you'll get to eat."

"I wanna change and touch up my makeup," Ryan declared.

Jake sat down with his sandwich and propped his feet on the adjacent chair. "Derek can show you around."

Jason, Derek, and their dates went upstairs with their bags. Ben walked over to Claire, who had situated herself in the sitting area before the fireplace.

"Something to drink?" he asked her.

She nodded.

"There's water, tea—"

"You her fuckin' waiter?" Jake sneered.

Going to the kitchen, Ben poured a glass of water and set it before Claire. She gave him a look of gratitude.

"You're not trying to starve your slave?"

"Hey, you worry about your slut, I'll worry about mine."

"I'd want to make sure mine had enough stamina."

"You gotta teach them their place first."

Ben walked over to the table but stood before the windows. "Is that why you have them sleeping in the basement?"

"You got it. Where's Slut #2?"

"Taking a nap in my room."

Jake shook his head. "You're starting off on the wrong foot. Better to be hard on them at the beginning, then they appreciate it when you're kind. You start off wussy, they won't learn proper submission."

"You don't have to be an asswipe about it."

Jake bristled. "You got your way, I've got mine. Besides, women *want* this. They want a man to totally dominate them and tell them what to do. I'm just giving them what they want."

"How come they didn't come with anything?"

"No time to pack, but it's not like they're going to need clothes here."

"They look tired."

Jake slowed his chewing as he stared at Ben. "What's it to you?"

"What do you know about these women?"

"All I need to know. The Scarlet Auction takes care of testing them for STDs, and the women fill out questionnaires about what they like and shit."

"You get to see the questionnaires?"

"Yep. I only go for women that are game for just about anything. Your slut, for example, indicated she's into hardcore BDSM."

Ben felt his pulse quicken at the prospect, but he wasn't ready to take anything Jake said at face value. "Do you have the questionnaire for Montana?"

"Who? Oh, you mean Slut #2. Nah, I left the printouts at the auction."

Ben half suspected Jake hadn't read any of it. "What do the women get to know about you?"

"Nothing. It's an auction, not a matchmaking service."

"What happens if they decide they don't want to go through with something?"

Jake shrugged. "They can call it quits, but they won't get their money then."

Jake crumpled up his sandwich wrapper and tossed it at the wastebasket with a pretty good hook shot.

"Tyrell call you back?" Ben asked.

"Nope."

"Try him again."

"What's your hurry?"

Ben wanted to finish his business with Jake sooner rather than later. He didn't want to spend the whole week with the guy.

"My dad called asking for an update."

"Fine," Jake grumbled before pulling out his cell to make the call.

Ben only overheard the beginning of the conversation because he saw *her* at the top of the stairs. She was wearing his shirt and sweatpants and looking damn sexy in them. The sweatpants had drawstrings, and she had rolled up the bottoms, otherwise they would have been too long on her. Her full curls, no longer half straightened, were swept back in a hair tie, and she had removed her makeup. Their gazes met, and he was struck by how bright her eyes were.

Holding her half-eaten sandwich, she glanced over at Claire several times as she descended the stairs. He met her at the bottom. The bruise on her cheek had darkened in color, but the swelling had gone down.

"Thank you for the nap," she said.

"Glad you got some rest," he replied.

She stared at him with enough intensity, he almost shifted his weight. She was sizing him up again.

"Should I call you Ben or Master?" she asked.

"Ben for now. I'll let you know when things change."

She stiffened but gave a curt nod. She looked over at Claire. "Do you mind if I talk to her?"

"Go ahead."

He was ready to change out of his suit but decided against leaving the two women alone with Jake. He watched Montana approach Claire and put a hand on her shoulder.

"You doing okay?" she asked Claire.

Claire nodded.

"You want a turkey sandwich?"

"Hey!" Jake snapped to Ben. "Your slut's not allowed to talk to mine unless I say it's okay."

Ben put his hands on his hips. "She's just giving her a sandwich."

Jake glared at Montana. "Fine. I was going to let her eat anyway."

"So what did Tyrell say?"

"China's not his first choice, obviously, but he's willing to hear some numbers."

"Two and a half million for a two-year deal. One-point-one million if it's going to be one year."

"You can do better than that. Marbury made two mill on one year."

"Marbury is a beloved celebrity in Beijing. Nobody's heard of Tyrell."

"Make it one-point-three million."

Ben thought it over. "Set up an in-person meeting, and I'll consider it."

"What, you don't trust me to deliver the message?"

"Just set up the meeting."

Jake rolled his eyes. "I'm gonna go take a shower. Come on, Slut #1, you're shaving that bush of yours. I don't like my slaves hairy."

Claire dutifully scurried after Jake. Ben looked over at Montana.

Finally, they were alone.

CHAPTER NINE

Kimani watched Ben move over to the bar. She still didn't know what to make of him. He had a very serious demeanor but seemed nice enough. After all, he had let her nap and given her clothes, and he hadn't made her give him a blow job — yet. But maybe anyone seemed nice next to Jake. And how good a guy could he be if he was willing to pay for sex? It wasn't like a guy with his assets would have a hard time getting laid, which made the fact that he would pay for sex all the more disgusting.

"Red or white?" he asked as he perused the wine bottles.

"I don't drink."

He looked at her. "At all?"

"I mean, I'm not much of a drinker. I drink a little now and then."

He selected a bottle of Buena Tierra Vineyard from the Russian River Valley. He popped the cork. "Half a glass won't hurt you, and it might take the edge off your nerves."

He could tell she was on edge? She accepted a glass from him, reminding herself that she had a role to play, and maybe if she drank, he would, too. He seemed guarded, and she had to loosen him up to get him to talk. While in his room, she had gone through his luggage, but all she'd found were clothing, toiletries, and a laptop and iPad, both password protected.

"Thanks for letting me borrow some clothes," she said after a moment of silence.

"If you need anything, let me know."

"Thank you."

Looking at the stool at the end of the bar, she wondered if she should sit down. She wanted to launch into a number of questions but didn't want to appear too nosy.

He pulled the stool out for her. Gingerly, she sat down. He remained standing, his posture impeccable. It was too bad such a hot-looking guy was likely a lech, taking advantage of women who needed money.

She took a sip of the chardonnay and was immediately taken by its brightness and apple-blossom aroma.

"I usually prefer Italian whites, but the Russian River Valley wines have grown on me," Ben said as he studied the wine's coloring.

"Are you a wine aficionado?"

"No. Like you, I'm not much of a drinker. Sake is usually my alcohol of choice if I feel like drinking."

She was glad to hear he didn't drink much and hoped that meant he wouldn't try to get her drunk. Silence followed as she wondered if she could ask to use his cellphone. She wanted to text or call Sam so badly.

"Something wrong?"

Realizing she had been fiddling with the stem of the wineglass, she met his gaze. She had to ask, and if there were repercussions, then she would know he was an asshole just like Jake.

"I was wondering…if I could use your cellphone?"

"You didn't bring yours?"

"I think the auction staff might have taken it."

"Why would they do that?"

"I don't know, but both Claire and I had phones, and now they're gone."

He pulled out his cell, unlocked it, and handed it to her. She nearly jumped for joy. Should she call or text Sam? Since she couldn't be sure he wouldn't listen in on her conversation, texting would be safer. She started typing as quickly as she could:

Sam, it's Kimani. Was bid on and taken to remote lakeside cabin. Trinity County, I think. My cell was taken. I'm okay at present. Will text again.

After pressing send, she breathed a sigh of relief. At least now Sam might have a way of tracking her down if he didn't hear from her.

"Done?"

"Yes, thanks," she replied, handing Ben back his phone, then realized she should have deleted the text.

"So tell me about yourself," Ben said. "All I know about you is that you play ball, don't drink much, and have a communications degree from Stanford."

He wanted to know about her? At least he realized she was a human and not just an object for sex.

"Not much to tell," she answered. "You seem like a more interesting person."

He didn't take the bait. "I'm not that interesting."

She shook her head. "Typical Asian modesty."

He raised his brows, and she immediately regretted her words.

"I'm sorry, I didn't mean to offend," she apologized. "I meant it as a compliment. It's just that my friends at school, the Asian ones, they never bragged. My sophomore roommate was from Singapore, and every time I paid her a compliment, she would talk about how terrible she was at something. It got so I was better off criticizing her than complimenting her."

For the first time, she thought she detected a smile tugging at one corner of his lips. It made him look irresistible, and she had to remind herself that he just might be a better form of asshole than Jake.

"While modesty is valued in my father's culture, it's not universal," Ben said. "The Chinese word for China is 'Middle Kingdom' because China believes it is the country between heaven and earth."

"Are you from China?" she asked. He had a hint of an accent, but it wasn't necessarily Eastern.

"I was born there, but my father sent me to boarding school in England when I was in my teens."

"Where'd you go to college, before Stanford that

is?"

"Howard University."

She did a double take. "Seriously? You went to Howard?"

He smiled to himself. "To be honest, I did it to piss off my dad. He wanted me to go to Harvard. So now that I've told you something about me, it's your turn."

His stare pinned her in place. She took a gulp of wine. Somehow, they had fallen into easy conversation, almost as if they were on a date.

"What—what do you want to know?"

"How old are you?"

"Twenty-five."

"Are you a virgin?"

"Say what?"

"I don't have the benefit of the questionnaire you filled out for the auction."

"Oh."

Here it goes. The sex.

"That's kind of a personal question," she stalled.

"This isn't a job interview. Or a date."

Right. What happens if he wanted a virgin? Would he toss her back to Jake if she told the truth? What sick fuck only wanted to do it with virgins?

"Do you prefer virgins?" she asked.

"Are you looking to be disciplined?"

Her mouth went dry.

"Look, this'll go a lot easier if you just answer my questions."

"No, I'm not a virgin."

He looked relieved. "I understand you're into BDSM?"

She hesitated, wondering what the best answer was. On the one hand, she didn't want to engage in sex, let alone BDSM sex with a stranger. On the other hand, she didn't want to risk being returned to Jake if that's what Ben was looking for. "It depends..."

"On what?"

"On the guy."

"Do you have any hard limits?"

Everything is off limits to perverts who prefer to pay for sex. But she couldn't blow her cover, and in truth, her mind drew a blank. If he was a halfway normal super-sexy guy, she would have been open to trying just about anything. Still, there was something about him that messed with the logical part of her brain, and so she answered stupidly.

"Maybe."

"You can't think of any off the top of your head?"

"Like I said, it depends on the guy and how comfortable I am."

She felt a little better with that statement, like she had salvaged some of her IQ.

"What would you like your safety word to be?"

The question stumped her. She had never had a safety word before because she had never delved into any hardcore stuff. She and one of her ex-boyfriends had played around with rope, spanking, and a crop, but otherwise, most of the sex she'd had was vanilla.

"What do you usually use?" Ben prodded.

"I don't…it's been a while, so…"

"Mercy. Your safety word is mercy."

Feeling a lump in her throat, she only nodded. Jesus, she had better get the info she needed and get out of here. Sooner rather than later.

CHAPTER TEN

So you got yourself a pretty cute chick," Jason said to Ben as they stood in the living room while Derek mixed drinks at the bar and the women chatted amongst themselves out on the patio. He passed Ben a joint.

Feeling more relaxed now that he had changed into a gray t-shirt and pair of jeans, Ben took a hit and returned it. "Calling women 'chicks' is such a nineties thing. Maybe an eighties thing."

"Hey, you used to talk like that, too."

"Yeah, *used* to."

"Anyway, I'm glad you changed your mind. Like I said, I would've considered sharing Lisa, but it's better you got your own fucktoy."

Ben glanced at Lisa, whose stick figure reminded him of a pre-pubescent girl. His gaze went to Montana—or Kimani, rather. He had discovered her name when he'd opened his phone and saw the text she had sent. Even though she looked just as hot in his shirt and sweatpants as any of the other three barely dressed women, a part of him couldn't wait to see her naked again. She didn't have model-perfect proportions, but she possessed a confidence in her body that was as sexy as anything.

Derek handed out the drinks, which Kimani declined.

"My chef is away because his wife is in labor," Jake announced, "so I sent Vince to get pizza. Tomorrow, one of you sluts is responsible for making lunch and dinner."

"I don't cook," Lisa replied.

"Neither do I," Ryan echoed. "I can maybe make Ramen if you have any around."

"Well, you're gonna have to learn to cook or suffer the consequences," Jake said. "I'm gonna lay down some ground rules here. This is how it works in my cabin. You sluts do whatever the fuck we tell you. You sleep downstairs. You call us Master—each and every fucking one of us. And if you're good sluts, you'll get rewarded. If not, you get punished."

Kimani's jaw tightened.

"So live it up while you can tonight. Tomorrow, we get serious," Jake finished. He wrapped his arm around Claire, who was wearing a skirt and top borrowed from Ryan. "Right, slut?"

"Yes, Master," she answered.

Lisa draped an arm over Jason's shoulder. "Can't wait for the fun to begin. *Master.*"

After getting two glasses of water, Ben walked over to Kimani, who stood by the porch railing. Against the backdrop of the sun setting behind the lake, with the sky colored by vibrant orange and pink hues, she looked like something out of a romance flick.

Accepting the water, she seemed a little surprised.

"Thank you. You're not going to try to get me drunk?"

"The way I play, it's best the sub retain all her faculties," he said.

Her lashes gave a quick flutter, and she drank the water as if it were alcohol she needed to fortify her nerves.

"Are you suggesting you play...hard?" she asked.

"I've never read that *Fifty Shades* book, but a date told me all about it. Let's just say that Christian Grey sounds like a tame little puppy."

"You get off on inflicting pain on women?"

He returned a cool stare. There was heat in her tone. If she was open to BDSM, why did she ask such a question?

"If *she* does, then yes," he replied.

"If she doesn't, then you wouldn't?"

"That would be logical."

"So, if a woman didn't want to do a particular thing, you wouldn't make her?"

"Why do you ask?"

"It's just that your buddy Jake said we're supposed to do whatever the fuck you tell us."

"He's not my buddy. But I thought that's what you signed up for?"

"What if I changed my mind?"

Shit. It wasn't what he wanted to hear. "Changed your mind about what?"

She took a deeper breath. "About sex with a stranger."

"Do you have a problem with that?"

"Not exactly."

"Sex with a stranger isn't something new, is it?"

She narrowed her eyes. "I take it it's not new for you?"

He held her judgmental stare. "I asked you first."

"I may have had a one-night stand or two—back in college. When I was a horny eighteen-year-old."

"Are you saying you're not horny anymore?"

She bristled. "Sex just isn't as big a deal anymore."

"That's too bad."

She bristled even more. "I'm busy now. I've got a career and rent and student loans to pay."

"Luckily, you've got this week to make up for your abstinence."

"I didn't say I was a monk and haven't had any sex since college."

"Good to know."

She shook her curls in indignation. It was almost too cute.

"Your turn," she snapped. "You've had a lot of one-night stand with strangers?"

"That wasn't the original question, but yes, I've had one-night stands with strangers. I don't know if your definition of 'a lot' is the same as mine. But, like you, I'm busy. One-night stands are easier. I'm not looking for a relationship right now. I take it you aren't either."

"Of course not! Especially…"

"Especially what?"

"Especially with guys who pay for sex. I mean, it's

obvious men who pay for sex aren't looking for a relationship—not the healthy, loving sort, anyway. This is just a business transaction, right?"

"You sound like you have a problem with that."

"I do—I mean, I don't."

"You said that if a guy has a right to buy sex, a woman should have the right to sell it."

"Sure, but that's just to be fair. Something about it doesn't feel quite right."

"That's because, throughout history, *men* have defined morality. And it suited our purpose to have women value chastity."

She stared at him with her mouth agape. She had such lush lips, lips that he wanted to crush beneath his.

"Did you grow up in California?" he asked.

"Yes."

"I take it you're pro-choice."

"Damn right."

"Your body, your choice."

"Shouldn't you get to do with your body whatever you want?" he pressed.

"Yes, but...sex has been used for so long as a weapon to keep women down, to cheapen and objectify us. You're suggesting prostitution is somehow empowering?"

He took a step closer to her. "Shed the expectations of a patriarchal society for a minute and think about what *you* want, what you like. Do you like sex?"

Damn it. Her lips were still parted. And he was close enough to pull her to his body.

"S-Sure," she said. "When I choose to have it. And if he's—if the guy is attentive and knows what he's doing."

He lowered his voice. "Trust me. I know what I'm doing."

She seemed to swallow with difficulty. "How can I trust you? I barely know you."

"You have your safety word."

"And you'll honor it?"

He was being drawn into her vortex, eager to be close enough to feel her breath, but her doubt pulled him out. "Of course."

"So what if I said I wasn't up to doing anything at all?"

"At all? Like you want to leave and go home?"

"Yeah."

He rubbed his chin, where his five o'clock shadow was coming in. He felt like she was testing him. "Then you should leave and go home."

"And you'd let me go?"

He gave a wry look. "You think I'd force you to stay? That would be kidnapping."

Was she into kidnapping fantasies? Is that why she was asking? Or was she really having second thoughts?

"I *feel* like I've been kidnapped. I wasn't told I was coming here, and I don't know how to get back home. I kind of doubt I can get Uber out here. I don't even know where 'here' is."

He let out a long breath. "If you need a ride back,

my jet is at the Weaverville Airport. It can fly you to SFO."

Her eyes lit up. "You're serious? You'd let me go? What about the money you paid to Jake? I'm not sure he'd want to refund any of it."

"That's my problem. I'll figure it out."

She was silent in thought. When she met his gaze, she seemed less guarded. "You weren't at the Scarlet Auction. Why?"

"You asked me that already."

"You didn't supply an answer."

He went through his memory and realized she was right. "I had better things to do with my time."

"Like what?"

"That's a nosy question."

"What made you change your mind?"

"About what?"

"About bidding…on me."

He finished off his water. "Isn't it obvious?"

She shook her head. He tucked a curl that the breeze had blown into her face back behind her ear. The whites of her eyes were so bright, and despite the fact that the sun had set, her eyes glimmered. He cupped her jaw and drew her to him till his mouth was near her ear. His tone was low and hushed.

"I want to fuck you. I want to do you till you can't walk for weeks, torment you with a rapture that will have you sobbing. In short, I'm going to devastate you."

CHAPTER ELEVEN

*H*oly sweet Jesus.

Her jaw hit the floor. The guy didn't mince words, and they kept ringing in Kimani's head as her heartbeat jumped madly around at his touch.

I want to fuck you…do you…torment you…devastate you.

Of course, she knew he wanted sex. Why else would he have laid down two hundred thousand for her? In fact, it had been stupid of her to ask, like she was fishing for compliments. She had wanted to find out how different he was from Jake, but what had she expected he would actually say?

She shouldn't have asked because now her whole body had liquefied. If a saber tooth tiger were to jump out at her, she'd probably still be rooted to the spot, reduced to a gelatinous mess because of a few little sentences. It wasn't just the words, however. It was the way he had said them. And the fact that he was so close to her, making her pulse skittish. He smelled good. Not from a heavy cologne. Just a hint of his aftershave, the soap he used, and something that was him. Pheromones, maybe.

"Pizza's here," someone announced.

Pulling back, Ben let his hand drop from her jaw. It was then that she realized she had been holding her breath.

"Thank God," Ryan said. "Weed makes me famished."

"Sluts get to eat over there." Jake pointed to the coffee table before the fireplace.

Jason gave Lisa a slap on the rear as she stumbled with Ryan and Claire back inside the house.

Kimani didn't want to leave Ben. He was different from Jake. She had already seen evidence of that, and she believed him when he said he wouldn't hold her hostage. She hadn't expected to dip into a discussion of feminist political theory. When they were conversing, it had seemed like the others had faded away. There was so much more to Ben that she wanted to learn. And the way he stared at her, with such penetration, she felt naked in body and soul.

Kimani bet a lot of other women melted instantly under his gaze, but she shouldn't give in so easily. Men with his kind of wealth probably thought everything was theirs for the plucking, that they could buy anything they wanted, and women were ready to give it to them because society equated wealth with power. How different could he be?

She wanted to find out...but sensed herself at the edge of a cliff. It was dangerous, not because she might get pushed or slip and fall over the precipice. But because she might decide to leap.

Pulling herself away from the edge, she told herself

that she needed to talk more with the other women, especially Claire. Doing her best to contain her wobbly legs, she went inside the house. Before joining the other women around the coffee table, she took a large breath and shook Ben's words out of her head.

"I get the feeling Jake's going to make us eat out of dog bowls next," Kimani remarked as she knelt down at the table.

Ryan chuckled. "I wouldn't mind. He's so cute, I'd do anything he wanted."

"OMG, Montana, your guy is so hot, too," Lisa said as she helped herself to the cheese pizza.

Kimani glanced at Ben, admiring how his shirt fit over broad shoulders and revealed his muscled arms. He was chiseled but not beefy. She wondered briefly if she would get to see him without a shirt.

Girl, what is wrong with you? She snapped her attention back to the women.

"So you aren't nervous at all about this week?" she asked.

"Why should we be? Jason's a cute guy, and he's got a sense of humor. Honestly, your guy looks kind of serious, but I'd jump his bones in a second anyway."

"I'm just glad we weren't won by one of those old guys," said Claire. "I mean, most of the guys in the audience were so *old*."

"Most wealthy men in the world are on the older side," Kimani said. "They're only younger in fiction."

"Older men don't bother me. I mean, I'd rather marry an older rich guy than a younger poor guy," said Ryan. "I wasn't meant to live a poor lifestyle. Who wouldn't want to shop at Neiman Marcus and drive a Porsche if they had the chance?"

"But you don't necessarily need a man to do that."

"Who you kidding, honey? I'm not rich, and I don't know if I'll ever strike it a rich. It's much easier to marry or date rich."

"I don't care so much if a guy is rich," said Lisa, "as long as he's good-looking and good in bed."

"But fairy tales can come true where you have it *all*: a guy who's good-looking *and* rich," Claire interjected.

"What about a guy who's smart and caring?" Kimani asked.

"Of course he's got to be caring and totally in love with me," Lisa said.

"Smart as in book smart?" Ryan asked. "I don't date nerds."

"And nice," Kimani added, glancing at Claire. "Not a jerk."

"Depends how you define jerk," Ryan replied. "If he's arrogant and a little pushy, I can put up with that. But a cheating jerk, that's harder…well, men are *wired* differently. I mean, if some skank goes all out to seduce your man, he can't help his biology."

"What about a jerk who hits you when you don't do what he says?"

"Hits you how?"

Deciding it was best that the others knew more rather than less about Jake, Kimani lowered her voice. "Jake hit me on the cheek when I wouldn't go down on him."

"Jake? But I thought Claire was his?"

"He bid on me and Claire at first. Then, when Ben arrive, Jake sold me to Ben."

"How romantic," Lisa sighed.

"I don't think romance is the intent of the week. They're just after sex."

Ben's words echoed again through her head, making her shiver.

"Doesn't mean they can't fall in love," said Claire.

"Really? Jake *assaulted* me." Kimani stopped short of saying that she could press charges against him.

"I think he was just playing the dominant. You know, being super alpha."

"He called me a nigger."

"Maybe he thought he was being hip, like a rapper."

"Stop worrying so much," Ryan told Kimani. "You're being kind of a drag. Relax and have fun."

At that, Kimani decided to focus on her slice of pizza. Maybe Derek and Jason were decent guys, and that's why Lisa and Ryan weren't worried. But Kimani didn't think Jake was acting one bit. Was Claire that smitten with her fantasy that she couldn't see it?

Jason came over then and pulled Lisa onto the sofa with him. He had a glass of champagne for her. Taking the glass, she snuggled up to him. Seconds later, they were lip-locked.

"Hey, Slut #3!" Derek called from outside. "Get your ass over here."

Ryan got up and walked out to the patio. Jake came over next. He shot Kimani a smug look.

"You missed out," he said as he unzipped his pants.

Kimani felt her stomach plummet. He pulled out his cock and waved it in front of her. If she could be assured of not getting hurt, she'd bite his fucking dick off.

"Tell her how good this tastes," he commanded Claire.

"It tastes good, Master," Claire said.

"I bet you want to suck it bad."

"I do, Master."

Jake smirked at Kimani. "What do you say? Wanna taste?"

She stared at him, fighting the urge to show her disdain, but her mother didn't bring her up to back down. Straightening her shoulders, she retorted, "I'd rather puke."

The vein at his temple throbbed. He grabbed her by the ear, wrenching her to him as he lowered his head to say something.

"Did I say you could touch my sub?"

Jake looked up, and seeing Ben, released her.

"Your slut's being a bitch," he spat. "I was just going to teach her some manners."

"That's my prerogative."

Ben jerked his head at Kimani to indicate she should follow him. She scrambled to her feet, eager to get away from Jake, and walked out to the patio with

Ben. With night falling, the temperature had cooled. A couple of the heat lamps had been lit. Over at a patio table, Derek and Ryan were making out. Derek had pulled down Ryan's tank top, exposing her lacy bra.

Ben took a seat on a lounge chair. "Sit down."

She looked around for the nearest chair.

He indicated his lap. "Here."

She sucked in her breath. It was time. The edge of the cliff loomed. He hadn't asked for sex so far, but everyone else was going at it. Glancing inside, she saw that Lisa had rolled on top of Jason, and Claire was giving Jake another blow job.

Could she do it? Should she do it?

Torment you with rapture...devastate you...

She didn't want to get sent home. Not when her story was incomplete. Gingerly, she sat down on his legs, but closer to his knees than his pelvis. Her body was turned perpendicular to his, so she could easily hop off if he tried anything. She hoped he wouldn't. Right?

"Are you trying to piss Jake off?" he asked.

She thought for a minute. "Maybe."

A grin tugged at one corner of his mouth.

"He was being an asshole," she explained.

"He's a Dom, you're a sub. I thought you knew how things worked?"

"He's not *my* Dom."

"Then let me handle Jake."

He ran a thumb beneath the bruise on her cheek. Did he know that Jake had hit her?

"Do you hit your subs if they don't snap to?" she asked, hoping her voice didn't quiver because of his touch.

"Some women like to be slapped around—"

"In play. No one wants to be beat up in real life."

"Of course in play. There's nothing nonconsensual here. In fact, you're going to be begging for it all, even the punishments."

Her mouth went dry, but she managed a doubtful laugh, though it sounded more insecure than confident.

His fingers curled around her neck. His hand felt warm and strong. Suddenly every inch of her skin had come to life.

"Do you like to be slapped around?" he asked, his thumb now tracing below her bottom lip.

Her words came out breathier than she intended. "I don't think so."

Don't think so? The answer should be n-o!

His fingers massaged the back of her neck, and when she met his gaze, molten with desire, she tried to pull herself from the whirlpools of his eyes. She should stop this, explain she was still nervous, suggest he see how she felt tomorrow. But, Jesus, his hand felt so good.

It dropped lower, to the muscles that ran below her shoulders. She nearly purred as he worked the tension away.

"This isn't your first massage," she murmured.

He didn't say anything, just pulled her to him till

she rested against him with her head upon his chest.

Stop it now before it's too late, a voice inside her warned. *Just because he's nicer than Jake doesn't mean he's safe to be with.*

His fingers dipped into her shirt to work her upper back. His touch was firm, the perfect amount of pressure. Beneath her, she felt the rise and fall of his chest, heard the sound of his heart beating.

I'm supposed to be working on a story, not succumbing to one of the subjects!

The massage went on for a while, but she wasn't stupid. This wasn't a massage for the sake of a massage. This was a massage that was going to lead to sex.

And it was a long way down from the edge of the cliff.

CHAPTER TWELVE

Ben breathed in the coconut and almond scent from the shampoo she had used. She smelled good. Clean and refreshing. Not like Lisa and Ryan, who had drenched themselves in floral perfume.

She felt good, too. He liked her sturdy frame, which suggested she wouldn't break into pieces if he fucked too hard. His jeans had become tight over his wood, but he didn't do more than massage her shoulders and neck. Off in the back corner of the patio, Derek and Ryan were getting louder.

"Nice titties," Derek was saying.

Ben had seen Kimani's baps when Jake had her completely naked, and all the things he could do with her dark and beautiful nipples flashed through his mind.

"About tonight…" Kimani started.

"Shh. Don't fret about what's to come, just stay in the moment," he said. He sensed she wasn't as wary of him as she had been before, but she wasn't completely at ease. He didn't understand why she was so hesitant. Surely she knew the expectations of participating in the Scarlet Auction.

He continued to rub her back and shoulders as if

she were a child in need of soothing. It wasn't easy when he wanted to rip off her clothes and go to town on her body.

"What kinds of things turn you on?" he asked. Conversation would distract him from focusing on the way her ass curved into him.

"I should probably tell you, I've never done anything like the Scarlet Auction. This may take some getting used to."

"We're just making conversation. I want to know what things turn you on."

She was quiet at first before answering, "Lots of different things."

"Like what?"

"Like... sexy lingerie, good foreplay... Idris Elba..."

Shit. How was he going to top Idris Elba? At least she wasn't entirely immune to Benjamin Dmitri Lee. He had sensed it. Her breath had stopped when he'd told her he wanted to fuck her. Maybe it was shock, but there wasn't just fear in her eyes. There was interest. And arousal.

"What do you imagine doing with Idris Elba?"

"I don't have any specific fantasies. He's an engaged man."

"If he wasn't, what would you want him to do to you?"

"Anything." She turned the question on him. "What turns *you* on?"

"When I was younger, I had a crush on the actress

Gong Li."

At the moment, you *are what turns me on. The vision of you tied to the bed, naked, screaming out my name. You tied in strappado with my cock banging you from behind.*

"What's the best orgasm you've ever had?" he asked before his imagination made his erection too painful.

"My first time with a vibrator. I had no idea they could be so...powerful."

"How about recently?"

"I love the combination of my Hitachi and a pair of Ben Wa balls."

He stored that bit of information away.

"Your best experiences have been with a vibrator, not a guy," he noted.

"Hate to break it to you," she murmured, "but that's the case with a lot of women."

"Well, that's about to change. For you, anyway."

She stiffened slightly. "You think you're all that?"

It was said with a nervous laugh.

"I do."

"How do you know your confidence isn't misplaced?"

"Experience."

"Most women won't offer up complaints because they don't want to hurt anyone's feelings."

"The women I've fucked come back for more."

"Sure they do, especially when you pay them."

"You're the only one I've ever paid for."

She cleared her throat. "These experiences of

yours, are they a good sample size?"

"You want stats? I haven't run a regression analysis, but practice makes perfect. And I've had a lot of practice."

"So you're slutty as well as cocky?"

"What is it with black women and sass?"

"Hey, that's a stereotype, a trope perpetuated by the media."

"Don't get me wrong. I like your sass. It makes me want to fuck you more."

Her body squirmed. In an instant, his pants became a painful cage. He resorted to talking again.

"If I was going to see any action at Howard, I had to be good. You know what they say about black men: they're better hung and better lovers. How was I going to compete with that? I had to up my game, and practice was the way to do it."

One of the few things going for him as a freshman at Howard was the ratio of women to men. Women outnumbered men nearly two to one.

"Yeah?" she challenged. "If you've had all that practice, you should have discovered that everyone is different. What works for one woman won't necessarily work for another."

"Don't worry. I'll find out everything that works for you."

Her breath had become uneven. They could both hear Ryan and Derek grunting. She gasped when he shifted her so that she lay on her back instead of her side. Her arse was now fully pressed against his pelvis.

Reaching around her, he cupped a breast. He caressed the contour of the delicious orb. She gasped loudly when he passed over her nipple.

"Sensitive?"

He passed his hand back over the nipple, making her gasp again. The bud hardened beneath the shirt.

"Let's start with your baps."

"My what?"

"Your tits." He began kneading the flesh. "Do you like that?"

"Umm…"

He watched the heaving of her bosom. Heat roiled in his balls. She yelped when he tugged her nipple lightly. It was going to be fun playing with these.

Her arousal now permeated the air about them, and he dared to lower his hand to cup her mound. She breathed in sharply but made no protest. He rubbed her through the sweatpants and was satisfied to feel dampness seeping through the fabric. With his free hand, he played with her other breast while the hand below continued to grope her.

"I shouldn't…"

It was a strange thing to say for a woman who had agreed to sell her body for money. He rubbed the fabric into her folds, making sure it grazed her clit. She released a soft moan.

"Oh, you're such a good fucking slut," Derek grunted while Ryan alternated between gasping and groaning.

"Really, we should…" Kimani tried.

He knew she was waging a losing battle. The natural desires of her body were going to overwhelm rational thinking. The more he stroked, the wetter she got.

Derek emitted a howl, evidence he had reached his climax. When it became quiet in that area of the patio, Ben almost wished Derek hadn't finished yet. For once, Derek's presence actually added something. Ben heard the sound of a lighter, then smelled the weed.

Several minutes later, Kimani began to writhe and tense in earnest. Tension tightened his groin. Her trembles made his blood boil. He made sure to slide his digits along the length of her clitoris. She whimpered, music to his ears. Her writhing grew bolder as she neared her climax.

"Oh, Jesus," she whispered, right before she came, gyrating all over his body.

He lightened but didn't stop his caresses, not until he had wrung the last of the spasms from her. Though his cock was harder than flint, he remained where he was. He had her where he wanted her. And he wasn't done.

CHAPTER THIRTEEN

Just as Kimani had feared, she had stumbled off the cliff. But how far down would she fall before she splattered on rock bottom?

She lay atop him, breathing deeply, her body tingling. A blissful warmth had flooded her and she didn't want to move, didn't want to think about any consequences that would follow. She had allowed a subject in her story to masturbate her. And now that she had come, what was he going to expect in return? She could feel his hard-on pressing against her rump.

He slid his hand into the sweatpants. The flesh-on-flesh contact startled her, but he secured her with his other arm. His fingers combed through her pubic hair till they reached the wet flesh below. Was he getting her ready to have sex with him? Maybe there was a chance to pull herself back onto the cliff? They had messed around, but she hadn't slept with him yet. Maybe he would be content with a hand job?

His fingers slid against the side of her clit, making her shiver. He found a spot that was still receptive to his touch. Very receptive.

Come on, Kimani, get it together.

Maybe this was what came of not having had sex in a while. A vibrator wasn't the same. There was

something scintillating about human touch—
especially his touch. Unlike a lot of men, Ben took his
time. He explored the terrain of her clitoris, hitting the
spots that made her moan. Occasionally his fingers
would graze her slit, and she found the possibility that
he might enter her exciting.

This is wrong, Kimani.

And that probably only made it more titillating. As
she warred with herself, his other hand fondled a
breast. She was trapped against him, his hands
working her erogenous zones. When he curled the tips
of his digits into her pussy, she lifted her hips to meet
him. Wetness gushed from her like she was a horny
teenager.

Slowly, he sank his fingers farther into her wet
heat. She let out a shaky breath when he withdrew his
fingers.

Dammit. What should I do?

Once more, he delved into her, telling her what she
should do is sit back and enjoy the ride. He stroked her
insides and caressed nerves that made her cry out,
almost laugh at the exquisiteness. Sometimes her Ben
Wa balls would hit that area, but his fingers were
constant, relentless. His other hand squeezed and
manhandled her breast. She yelped when he pinched
the nipple. Lust filled her head. She couldn't process
all the sensations assaulting her. The hand between her
legs was the dominant contributor to her frenzy. She
gripped the arms of the chair as if her life depended on
it.

"Oh, Jesus," she muttered through clenched teeth.

Her body didn't know whether to squirm or stay still, relax or tense, contract away or press into his hand. She wanted the impending orgasm, but she was worried, too. What if she couldn't handle it? What if...

His hand covered the whole of her breast. She cried out when he tugged her nipple harder while his other hand worked her tirelessly. Fingers curled inside her. Palm pressed to her clit.

Jesus. Now she felt like she needed to pee. Her knuckles turned white as she resisted the urge.

"Give in," he encouraged. "Your body wants to come."

The tension inside her had reached such heights that it would take hours to calm back down. The quickest way to relief was through explosion, but could she handle the force of it? What if she lost control of her body and pissed all over herself?

Must resist.

"Come for me, Kimani."

His words, perhaps the sound of her name, was the lever that unleashed the dam. Several gasping cries tore from her as her body bucked uncontrollably against him. He pulled his fingers out.

"Oh, fuuuuck," she sobbed as wetness gushed from her.

He plunged his fingers back in and caused another eruption to wave through her. He pulled out again, releasing another spray. As she feared, she had lost control of her body. But it was worth it, worth the euphoria that drowned her.

She lost track of how many times his fingers entered her. Her body quaked from the intensity. She couldn't catch a calm breath. The area between her legs wasn't just wet, it was sodden.

As he withdrew, his fingers grazed her clitoris, and she nearly shivered out of her skin. Control of her body lay in pieces about her. She stared into nothingness, feeling like a complete mess, a fucking amazing mess.

CHAPTER FOURTEEN

She was so unbelievably hot when she came, Ben thought to himself. He'd finger fuck her again if he thought her up to it. His cock was screaming for release, to sink itself into her super-wet furnace. It was going to feel like a piece of heaven when he did.

"I—I messed up your sweats," she whispered when she had recovered enough to talk. "I don't know what happened—I'm so sorry."

"Don't know what happened?" he echoed, perplexed. "Is this your first time squirting?"

"Oh…"

It was. Ben smiled. Well, well…

"You should drink something, stay hydrated," he suggested, sitting her up.

"Okay."

She seemed surprised when he got up. He adjusted himself, though it did little to diminish the discomfort of his erection. He wanted to fuck her so badly, but that wasn't part of his plan. Yet.

As he went to get her a glass of water, he noticed Derek was in a drugged stupor, Jason and Lisa were lying in post-coital embrace on the sofa, and Jake had lit a cigarette. From the looks of contentment on their faces, it was obvious all three guys had come. Ben helped himself to a shot of vodka to take the edge off the tension in his body, since he couldn't jack off right away and Bataar wasn't around to spar with. He walked back to the lounge chair where Kimani was sitting.

"Thanks," she said when he handed her a glass of water. She drank it down and seemed to be waiting for him to say something. When he didn't, she asked, "So, um, what's next?"

"What do you want to happen next?"

She was taken aback. "I get to decide?"

"For tonight. We can step into our appropriate roles tomorrow."

"So you don't…need anything?"

"Are you offering?"

She looked down, and he knew her answer. It didn't bother him that she wasn't ready for more. There was time.

"How did you know my name?" she asked.

"You got a text."

He pulled out his phone and showed the message that had come in just before Jake had grabbed her by the ear. The message read:

Kimani, this is Sam. Are you doing okay?

"Is Sam your boyfriend?" he asked.

"No, he's my —" She stopped herself before she

revealed who Sam was. "I mean, *she*. Sam is short for Samantha. She knows I did the Scarlet Auction and is just checking in. Do you mind if I call her back?"

She was lying. Or at least not being completely truthful. Maybe Sam wasn't just a boyfriend. Maybe Sam was a husband. Or if Sam was a "she," the woman had to be more than just a friend checking in.

"Go ahead."

She got up. "I'll just—I have to go to the bathroom."

Shortly after she left, Jake walked over.

"So, what's black putang like?" he asked.

"Pussy is pussy," Ben replied. "It's always sweet."

"I don't know about that. Some are downright nasty and stink like shit. But virgin pussy is always fresh. All that blood makes things nice and slick, too."

"You do your part right, you shouldn't need blood for lubrication."

"Yeah, but it's so erotic to see them coated in blood and shit."

Ben didn't bother asking what the "and shit" entailed. Instead, he asked, "So what happens after you pop their cherry? They won't necessarily bleed again for you, unless it's that time of month."

"Which is totally gross and not the same. Another reason the Scarlet Auction is so awesome. You don't have to worry about getting a menstruating girl. That shit's disgusting."

The conversation had reached the end of Ben's patience, but he had to ask one last question. "How's

Claire doing?"

"You mean Slut #1. She's doing great. She had two dinners, you know what I mean?"

Ben turned, ready to head inside.

"How's yours?" Jake asked. "She good at sucking dick? I bet black women are good at it. They got those naturally big lips."

Ben's right hand curled into a fist. "You set up that meeting with Tyrell yet?"

"Yeah, he's around next week if you're able to fly down to LA. What day is good for you?"

He remembered Kimani had his phone, so he couldn't check his calendar. "I'll get back to you."

He found the bathroom and was about to knock on the door when he heard Kimani. She was still on the phone.

"No, don't call or text me," she was saying, "not on this phone. It's not mine... It belongs to a guy named Ben. I don't know his full name, but I know he's involved with Chinese basketball, and he graduated from Howard University and the Stanford business school. There can't be that many Asians who went to Howard, then Stanford. Well, he's only part Asian— I'm guessing Chinese. He looks a little mixed, like Eurasian. He's working on some deal with this guy named Jake. I'm pretty sure that's his real name, or at least a nickname. He's some kind of sports agent. They talked about a basketball player named Tyrell Jenkins... Okay, you can let me know what you find when I call tomorrow."

Seconds later the bathroom door opened.

"Came to see how you were doing," he explained when his presence startled her.

"I'm good. About your sweats...I'll wash them or buy you a new pair."

He didn't tell her that the sweatpants she wore from Berluti sold for well over nine hundred dollars. "Don't worry about it."

Eying the wet stains on the sweats, he thought through his clothes. He didn't have anything else that wouldn't fall right off her hips, but the shirt she wore was long enough to cover her arse.

"Here's your phone." She handed it back to him. "Could I borrow it again tomorrow?"

He eyed her carefully. She was having this Sam person look him up. Possibly doing her due diligence and making sure he wasn't a convict or psycho. The NDA she must have signed with the Scarlet Auction might only have pertained to Jake. Nonetheless, if there wasn't already language there, a lawyer could probably make the case that the NDA extended to third parties.

"It's just that Sam will get worried if he — she doesn't hear from me."

Why was she covering up who Sam was?

"I don't care if you have a boyfriend, or even a husband." Especially if the guy was fully aware of what she was doing, like Woody Harrelson's character in *Indecent Proposal*.

"No, no," she quickly refuted. "I sometimes get my

pronouns mixed up because...Sam's a transsexual."

He took his phone back. "I'm not going to snitch on you if you lied to the Scarlet Auction that you were single."

"I didn't. I'm just used to referring to Sam as a 'he.' So, can I use your phone again tomorrow?"

"Sure."

"Thanks. Sam—*she* can be such a worrywart."

Ben let it go, even though something still sounded off about the whole thing.

"And while we're here, can you call me Montana? I'd rather people didn't know who I really was. It would be too embarrassing if anyone I knew found out. Sam's the only one who knows I'm doing this."

This Sam was pretty special in her life. Ben had a mind to do some background checking himself. He had Sam's phone number in his cell since she had texted and called him. If Ben made a few calls, he could get a hacker in Singapore to dig up Sam's identity, address, and more.

He cupped her chin and tilted her face so that she couldn't avoid his gaze. He wanted to see her reaction when he said, "I don't have a problem calling you Montana. But the name I'd much rather use is *my pet*."

CHAPTER FIFTEEN

Her legs weakened. Kimani could smell herself on his fingers, which were wrapped firmly — uncomfortably, actually — about her jaw. The pupils of his eyes, darker than any she had known, had constricted. His current demeanor reminded her that the cliff she wanted to climb back on was dangerously high.

"Would you like that?" he asked. "Would you like me to call you *my pet*?"

Not really. Or maybe. By him. In the context of BDSM role-playing. But she had the feeling his was a rhetorical question, and the only appropriate response she could come up with was:

"Yes, Master."

His features softened and he released her jaw, allowing her to breath. At least "my pet" was better than "Slut #2." Wasn't it? Maybe not. Maybe being referred to as an animal was more demeaning than being referred to as a whore.

"Time to get these sluts their beauty sleep," Jake announced as he walked into the house.

"I'm not done with mine," Ben said.

"You had your chance, Benny boy. I don't want to

have to lock up twice."

"If you don't mind," she said to Ben, "I'd like to go with the other women. If that's okay with you... Master."

He seemed to like it when she called him Master. He nodded. She breathed in relief. As wonderful as her orgasms had been, she wasn't sure she was up to another. She needed to get a safe distance from him before she allowed herself to slide farther down that cliff.

"Vince, take the sluts downstairs," Jake ordered Mr. Stern-Face.

Lisa turned to Jason. "I thought I was staying with you?"

Jason shrugged.

"But I left my suitcase upstairs."

"Vince has already moved it," Jake informed her.

"Master," Claire piped up, "I don't have a hairbrush, or even a toothbrush."

Jake rolled his eyes. "Vince can find you a toothbrush."

"And you can borrow my hairbrush," Ryan offered.

"Sleep well. You sluts have a lot of work to do tomorrow."

He grabbed his crotch suggestively. Kimani glanced at Ben, her savior in many ways because the last thing she wanted was to have to go down on Jake. She hadn't told Sam about being hit because he probably would have told her to come straight home.

She couldn't wait to hear what he had dug up about Ben and Jake.

After Claire and Kimani received toothbrushes and the women attended to their oral hygiene in the first-floor bathroom, they all followed Vince downstairs. Once he got to their room, he flipped on the light switch. Ryan's and Lisa's bags were by the second mattress.

"This is where we're staying?" Ryan asked. "It's a shithole."

Lisa wrinkled her nose. "There aren't even any windows."

"Sleep tight, ladies," Vince said as he closed the door behind him.

Kimani heard the lock engage.

"Part of the BDSM thing," Claire explained. "We're supposed to be the sex slaves."

"I don't remember anything like this in *Fifty Shades*," said Lisa.

"Well, Anastasia wasn't a sex slave," Ryan clarified.

"It doesn't bother you that *you* are?" Kimani asked.

"You've never fantasized about being a sex slave to some super-hot guy?"

"I have," Lisa answered. "It's pretty cool that I get to play out one of my fantasies. How often does that happen?"

"I guess I have a hard time with the concept of slavery," Kimani said.

"That's history. We're talking fantasy. It's

different."

"Even so." Kimani tried to imagine being Ben's sex slave. Not a real slave. Just pretending, role-playing. The thought wasn't as revolting as she would've expected. Was being his slave better than being his pet? Or was it essentially the same thing?

"How is his cock by the way?" Lisa asked a little shyly.

"I don't know. I haven't seen it yet."

The other three stared at her.

"Then what were the two of you doing?" Ryan chimed in. "You were screaming plenty loud."

Kimani blushed. "We were just—he masturbated me."

"That's it?" Claire asked, stunned.

"That's it."

"He didn't fuck you?" Ryan inquired.

"Or make you suck him off?" Claire added.

"That's weird."

"Maybe he's super small," Lisa suggested. "Being tall doesn't mean you're well hung."

"My guy's got a super-small dick," sighed Ryan. "And he sucks at foreplay. In fact, there was barely any."

"Jason tried his best to hold out for me but I could tell he was having a hard time, so I faked my orgasm. How's Jake?"

Claire answered, "He's got a pretty nice cock, I guess. He only had me do a blow job tonight."

Ryan looked at Kimani. "Sounds like you're the

only one among us who got to come. Lucky bitch."

After Kimani switched off the lights, they settled into bed, Ryan and Lisa on one mattress, and Claire and Kimani on the other.

"How was the rest of your time with Jake?" Kimani whispered to Claire.

"He took me out on his boat."

"Did you have fun?"

Claire didn't answer right away. "We had sex. It hurt a lot more than I expected, not like what I read in novels. Did it hurt the first time you did it?"

"Like hell. I remember thinking to myself that if this is what sex was like, I wasn't doing it again."

"But then it definitely gets better?"

"It gets a lot better. Especially with the right guy."

"Jake wouldn't let me wipe the blood away at first. He even licked it, like he was a vampire."

"Vampires are so sexy," Ryan said. "I wish vampires were real."

If they were real, they wouldn't be as sexy, Kimani thought to herself.

"Does Jake make you feel uncomfortable at all?"

"A little," Claire admitted," but I figure that's because it's just the first day."

"Well, if he makes you too uncomfortable, I've got your back. We're in this together."

Claire turned onto her side, away from Kimani, and was soon breathing deeply, leaving Kimani to her own thoughts. Her mind replayed snippets of her conversation with Ben and, of course, the way his hands had felt on her, in her. Without doubt, it had been one of the best orgasms she had ever had. At times she'd wondered if she *had* a G-spot, and now she knew. Jesus, it had felt so amazing. Squirting had felt amazing. Her body warmed at the memory, and her fingers wandered over the path his had tread. Would she get to have an orgasm again tomorrow? She rather hoped so.

Jesus, Kimani, did you forget you're working on a story?

Turning onto her side, she shoved her hands under the pillows. She wasn't here for sex, especially sex with a stranger. No matter how good-looking he was or how skillful his fingers were.

After waiting for the other women to fall asleep, she crept to her purse and pulled out a pen and her little notepad. There was a night-light plugged into a wall socket, and she jotted notes on everything that had transpired, except for the part where Ben had masturbated her.

Dammit. How could I have let this happen?

It was as if his massage on her, and even the sound of his voice, had lulled her into a trance, but she couldn't eschew responsibility and lay the blame at his doorstep. Simply put, she had allowed it to happen, had ignored her better judgment and surrendered to the rapture of his fondling.

By becoming involved with one of the subjects, she had likely compromised her story. She supposed she could give her account to another reporter so that the *San Francisco Tribune* could still get the scoop, but she herself wouldn't get the byline. She'd have to talk it through with Sam.

She put away the pen and notepad and crawled back into bed. Shutting her eyes, she willed herself to focus on sleep. And in her sleep, she dreamed of diving off cliffs.

CHAPTER SIXTEEN

The lake water was freezing, but Ben welcomed the cold because the morning swim helped cool his ardor after thinking about Kimani all night and first thing when he woke. Why the hell did he want her so badly? It was like he was back to being a horny teenager. He wanted her back on his lap, her body squirming atop his, his fingers buried in her hot, wet cunt. And they had just begun. There was so much more he could do, and he wanted to do it all.

He swam butterfly for 400 meters, then freestyle back to the shore. The final sprint had him nice and winded. With his heart pumping hard and the sun warming the water on his skin, he felt invigorated. He wrapped a towel around his waist and went up the stairs to the cabin.

While he was swimming, everyone else had risen. The guys were sitting around the dining table with bloody marys, Claire and Lisa were kneeling by the fireplace, and Kimani and Ryan were making breakfast in the kitchen.

Kimani was wearing her cocktail dress beneath his shirt. He smiled to himself to think the sweatpants might still be damp. She hadn't worn any panties beneath the sweatpants yesterday. Was she going commando right now? He imagined sliding his hand beneath her dress to find out.

"We're going out on the boat this morning for some skiing," Derek said to him. "You in?"

"Sure."

"Oh, wow," Ryan murmured after nearly bumping into Ben while carrying a plate of toast. Her gaze went up and down his bare chest.

Kimani, standing in front of the stove with a pan of scrambled eggs, looked over. Her gaze locked with his.

"Morning," he said.

"Morning," she replied, glancing over his body briefly before turning her attention back to the eggs.

"Good morning, *Master*," Jake told her before turning to Ben. "You got to do a better job teaching your slut proper sub behavior."

Ben took a celery stick to stay himself from saying something that would tick Jake off before the meeting with Tyrell had been set. "You worry about yours."

"You can't let them get away with the small shit, you know. Otherwise, they can get out of line and start topping from the bottom."

"Does that worry you?"

"Hell no. I just don't like it. Won't tolerate it. I was just giving you some friendly advice."

"I've been a practitioner for over ten years—"

Kimani nearly dropped the pan as she bobbled pouring the eggs onto a plate.

"—I know what I'm doing."

"Go put a shirt on," Jason said, throwing a kitchen

towel at him, "and stop showing off."

Glad to get away from Jake, Ben went upstairs to change. While in his room, he received a call from Stephens, who took care of special one-off projects for Ben.

"Rosenstein wants to know if you want to go with D. Brown, the younger consultant who knows Oakland well and has worked for several councilmembers," Stephens relayed, "or if you want Harris and Blume. Harris and Blume is a firm based in San Francisco but they have a lot of experience with independent expenditures."

"Goddamn it," Ben cursed. "You're not supposed to talk to me about the I.E. It can't coordinate with the candidate's campaign, and since I'm family, I'm considered part of Uncle Gordon's campaign."

"It was your idea to set up the I.E."

"But I can't run it, influence it, or communicate with it. I was clear with Rosenstein about that."

Rosenstein was a developer who the Lee family had worked with on a project not far from Oakland.

"Got it. I'll reinforce the message," Stephens acknowledged.

After finishing his call, Ben went downstairs to find that most of the guys had finished their breakfast. Jason was over by the fireplace with his hands down Lisa's tank top, Derek was making another drink, and Jake had gone out to get the boat ready.

Kimani set down a plate of eggs and toast on the table. "If you don't like your eggs scrambled, I can make them a different way."

"Did you eat yet?" he asked.

"We're supposed to wait until all the Masters have finished."

Taking a seat at the table, he indicated the chair opposite him. "Sit down."

She looked around before sitting.

He pushed the plate of eggs and toast to her. "Eat."

"Aren't you hungry?"

"I told you to eat."

He watched her pick up a fork and scoop a small amount of eggs into her mouth. He liked watching her eat. Occasionally, she would look up at him, and he wondered what was going through her mind.

He got up to make tea, then poured them both some orange juice.

"Thank you…Master."

The word didn't fall comfortably from her mouth, but a ripple went through his groin nonetheless.

"What about the Scarlet Auction appealed to you?" he asked. "You've got a Stanford degree. It's not like you can't get a job to make money."

She chewed her toast slowly and swallowed before answering. "Like I said, it's good money. And fast. I get paid within a week when everything's all done and over with."

"You need the money in a hurry?"

She shrugged. "I've got student loans to pay. I only had a partial scholarship to Stanford."

He narrowed his eyes. She had to be on a payment

plan for her student loans, so that hardly qualified as urgent. Maybe she had maxed out her credit cards. "So you don't have a job?"

"I have a job."

She sounded almost defensive.

"What do you do?"

She hesitated. "I work as an assistant."

"Where?"

"At a publishing house," she mumbled into her food. "The pay's not that great. It's expensive to live in San Francisco. Rents are through the roof, and they just keep getting higher."

"Your parents or family can't help you out with expenses?"

"I'm not going to ask my parents for help. They already dipped into their savings and retirement accounts to help pay for Stanford. They've done enough for me."

He was curious to know more about her family, her background, but that would be getting too personal.

"What about you?" she asked. "What do you do? Apart from paying exorbitant amounts of money for sex."

He leaned back to better view her. She said it half-jokingly, but there was an undercurrent of judgment there.

"My family's in real estate."

"What kind?"

"All kinds."

"Do you do mostly residential or commercial?"

"My father started with residential. Now it's a mix between the two."

"Where's the family business based?"

"We have offices in Hong Kong and Beijing."

"Do you live there?"

"Is this an interview of some kind?"

She lowered her lashes. "I was just curious. It'd be nice to know a little more about the guy I'm supposed to…you know…"

"The guy you're supposed to fuck?"

She looked him in the eyes. "Yeah. That."

"You make it sound like a chore."

"Well, I'm getting paid to do it."

"Doesn't mean you can't enjoy it. Was it a chore when you squirted last night?"

A blush colored her cheeks. She didn't seem to know where to look.

"I asked you a question," he said when it seemed she wasn't going to answer.

"No," she admitted. "But it's not always going to be like that, is it? I assume you've got…expectations."

"I've got a lot of expectations."

She swallowed. "What are they?"

"I'm not going to overwhelm you with them right now, but if you play your part right, last night won't be the only time you get to squirt."

Her lower lip hung agape, and it was all he could do not to reach over the table and capture her bottom lip with his mouth.

She reached for her orange juice and finished it.

"I'll fix up another plate for you."

He watched her walk into the kitchen, his gaze lingering on her booty. He wondered if she had ever had anal sex. That was one virginity he didn't mind taking. Feeling his groin tighten, he shifted in his seat and decided to look out the window.

The swim had made him hungry, and he ate everything she set down for him. She then brought plates over to the other women.

"You sure are nice to your slut," Derek said, taking a seat beside him.

"If you want a sub to go all out for you, if you want them to push their limits, you've got to build trust."

"Hunh," was Derek's response to something he clearly didn't understand.

Jake returned to announce the boat was ready. "Now you ladies get ready. Remember, I told you no clothes on the boat."

Lisa raised her hand.

"Put your fucking hand down. We're not in school."

"Permission to speak, Master," she requested.

"What is it?"

"What about swimsuits, like bikinis?"

"I said no clothes. That means nada, zilch, nothing."

The women looked at each other.

"So what are you waiting for?" Jake prodded.

"I don't mind skinny-dipping," Ryan said as she pulled off her top.

The others began to strip. Except for Kimani. Ben toyed with the idea of letting her out of Jake's directive, but decided against it. A little discomfort wouldn't hurt her. And he wanted to see how far she was willing to play.

CHAPTER SEVENTEEN

Kimani wanted to throw up. Yesterday was bad enough. Now there were four guys. To be naked in front of them, leered at, objectified. It was debasing and humiliating.

But that's how Jake wants you to feel, so don't give him the satisfaction.

But how could she not? It didn't seem as if Ben was coming to her rescue this time. He was watching her, gauging her.

She pressed her lips together. "Question, Master."

"Yes."

"What if I don't want to take off my clothes?"

Jake answered for Ben. "Then you stay behind."

Ben's silence confirmed the choice available to her. Staying behind wouldn't help with her story. She'd come all this way to do a deep dive into the world of the Scarlet Auction. She shouldn't let one asshole mess it up.

That's right, girl, own it.

Squaring her shoulders, she decided that Jake could objectify her in his eyes, but he wouldn't succeed in making her feel objectified. With or without clothes, she was beautiful and powerful. She was going to make *the choice* to be naked and proud.

She whipped off her shirt before she changed her mind, then unzipped the dress and stepped out of it. The women were sizing each other up, probably noting whose boobs were less than perky or whose butt was too big, but Kimani stared right at Jake.

He smirked before turning to Ben. "You ought to shave that bush of hers."

Ben, stone-faced, was about to step into Jake's space, but Jason intervened. "Maybe we can make that a group activity later."

"I already took care of my slut," Jake said, walking over to Claire and running his hand over her pubis. "Smooth as a baby."

"Come on," said Derek. "I want to get out on the lake before the wind picks up and the waves get choppy."

The men led the way out of the cabin and down to the dock. Vince was putting a cooler onto the boat.

"Where's the Malibu?" asked Derek. "I hate the wakes from a pontoon."

"Can't fit all of us on the Malibu, dipshit," Jake answered as he hopped onto the boat.

The boat before them was large enough to comfortably seat at least a dozen people, mostly in the front of the craft.

"Sluts up front," Jake ordered.

The women settled themselves in the plush seating. Derek stayed behind the helm since he would be the first to ski.

Though the scenery of blue water surrounded by

redwood trees was gorgeous, and the weather was a typical California summer with a sunny and cloudless sky, Kimani found it hard to enjoy the environment. She was a little disappointed Ben hadn't bailed her out, but she reminded herself that she was the lucky one of the bunch.

"Nice nipple ring," Jake said to Ryan, who seemed the most comfortable with her nudity. On her hip she had a tattoo of a heart and on her lower back she had a butterfly.

He moved to stand in front of Lisa and assessed her petite breasts. "Not bad. I can dig small."

When he got to Kimani, she ignored the churning in her stomach and lifted her chin. Jake glanced over at Ben and decided not to say anything. He tossed Claire a bottle of sunblock.

"You get to spread it on each other," he explained. "Wouldn't want you sluts getting sunburned."

Kimani made a silent groan. She often went without sunblock, especially the kind that didn't absorb well and sat like white paste on her darker skin. Claire squeezed some sunblock on her hand, then passed it to Lisa.

"I can do it," she said to Claire.

Jake gave her a wide grin. "Yeah, but you're not gonna."

She looked to Ben, who had taken a seat opposite her. Was he going to let Jake dictate everything? She had gotten the sense that Ben didn't care much for Jake.

"Be a good pet," he said.

Her heartbeat stumbled. It was not the response she wanted. She allowed Claire to apply sunblock to her arms but fumed inside. She wasn't as angry about having another woman touch her as she was with the fact that Ben was complicit with Jake and had called her a pet in front of everyone.

Jake hopped into the driver's seat and started the engine. Jason sat down next to Ben to enjoy the view of Lisa rubbing sunblock all over Ryan.

At first, Claire avoided the breast, pelvis, buttocks, and inner thighs.

"Make sure you apply it everywhere," Ben said.

Kimani frowned in his direction but said nothing when Claire rubbed the sunblock on the parts she had passed up earlier. It was weird to have a practical stranger touching her private parts, but Kimani treated it as a clinical experience no different from her annual visit to the gynecologist.

"Now return the favor," Ben directed when Claire had finished.

Getting some sunblock, Kimani took her turn. She didn't rush through it, deciding she preferred applying sunblock to Claire over whatever else the men might have in store for them.

"I get to even out my tan now," Claire said to Kimani. "It's like we're on the French Riviera."

Kimani looked at her own arms to see the sunblock hadn't seeped into the skin yet.

"Come here," Ben said. "I'll rub it in for you."

She didn't want to go over to him. She was miffed at him. He gave her a wordless look, and she suddenly felt like a petulant child.

"I'd rather not discipline you in front of everyone," he told her.

She sucked in her breath. What happened to the nice guy from yesterday? And what kind of discipline did he intend? Not wanting to find out, she stepped toward him.

"What's the matter?" he asked.

He was fairly intuitive for a guy, but she wasn't in the mood to acknowledge his better qualities. She replied, "You letting Jake be the alpha male now? He gets to dictate everything?"

Be chuckled as if he found her statement to be adorable nonsense. Pulling her closer, he began massaging the sunblock into her skin. Unlike the soft and light touch of Claire's hands, his were firm and hard.

"What did you think you were getting into when you signed up for the Scarlet Auction?"

She couldn't think straight when his hands were on her buttocks. "I don't know."

"You know how domination and submission works, right?"

Now his hands were on her thighs, perilously close to where they had been the night before. "Sure."

"Then tell me."

"It's a role-playing dynamic in which one person is in control and the other person submits to the one in control."

"And are you the sub?"

She glanced to see if anyone saw that she was being felt up, but Claire was sunbathing while completely reclined on the sofa, Ryan was watching Derek ski, and Lisa and Jason were making out. Ben turned her around.

"I suppose," she answered.

"The answer is yes. You are the sub. I am the Dom. So, like it or not, you do what I say. Unless you use your safety word."

Damn. She had forgotten she had a safety word. But would she have used it just now? Rubbing lotion on another woman or having it rubbed on her wasn't the worst thing in the world. In fact, it was no big deal. What she didn't like was that they were being ogled by the men while doing it.

Ben's hands were on her breasts now, his warm touch scattering her thoughts. She tried to rein them in.

"Now, what happens when you don't obey, when you're a bad pet?" he continued.

She searched his eyes but didn't find any malice. Nevertheless, her mouth went dry. "I get disciplined."

"I don't mind disciplining my subs, but I guarantee you'll like it better when I reward rather than punish."

"What—what do you do when you discipline?"

"That depends on the sub. Every woman is different. What's effective for one isn't necessarily motivating for another."

Putting a hand up to shield her face from the sun,

she narrowed her eyes. Was he deliberating parroting back what she had pointed out to him last night?

He removed the sunglasses he was wearing. "Here, take these and put them on."

"What for?"

"Do you question everything? Just do it."

Putting on the glasses, she was glad not to have to squint in the sunlight anymore.

"Jason, you want next?" Derek called when he reboarded the boat.

Jason and Lisa were busy necking, so Ben climbed over to the back of the boat. Kimani watched him peel off his shirt and put on a water-ski vest. After strapping on the skis, he grabbed the handlebar and jumped in the water. She had never been up close to water-skiing and was mildly curious, but mostly she kept thinking about her situation with Ben. She should never have let it get this far. She should have played up being nervous or shy and seen how far his patience would last. Now that she had allowed him access to her body, his expectations had clearly changed.

But how bad could being Ben's sub be?

"Nice shades," Ryan complimented. "Can I try them?"

Kimani handed them over.

"They're Louis Vuitton," Ryan cooed. "You're not impressed?"

Kimani shrugged. "They're sunglasses."

Shaking her head, Ryan handed her back the glasses. "Don't take this the wrong way, but you're a weird-ass chick."

"Why am I supposed to be impressed? So he can afford designer shades. Is he a better human being 'cause he's rich?"

"Uh, *yeah*. Money is power. It's the human equivalent of the stronger animal, the stag with the bigger horns, the peacock with the best feathers. And for us women, it's in our DNA to want the strongest, most powerful male. It's Mother Nature and evolution."

"But humans aren't just animals. We're evolved and enlightened. Frankly, I'd be more impressed with a guy who spends two years building water wells in Africa and *helping people* than a guy who can drop a thousand dollars on a pair of shoes and likes to make women feel like objects."

"Oh, honey, you sound like one of those feminist bitches who desperately need to get laid."

Kimani did a double take. "A feminist bitch?"

"Yeah, I can't stand feminists. They're always trying to make the rest of us feel bad."

Kimani was about to declare herself a feminist, but she had already talked too much. It wasn't the job of a journalist to voice her own opinions. In fact, doing so could dampen a subject from speaking openly.

She inquired, "So you're comfortable being paraded around naked?"

Ryan leaned back into the seating. "Sure. Women—not the cranky feminists, of course—don't mind being an object. It's sexy. Given the chance to pose naked for *Sports Illustrated*, we'd all do it. We want men lusting after our hot bods — unless you're a lesbo or a feminist. Basically they're one and the same."

"You're not bothered if men see us as objects instead of human beings with intellect, charisma, and heart?"

"That stuff's not real. If you believe all a guy cares about is your brains and personality, don't be surprised when you find out he's banging the slutty office intern." Ryan looked her over. "You've got a nice body. Flaunt it. Enjoy what you've been born with."

Ryan had spouted off some great quotes, and Kimani desperately wished she had brought one of her recording pens.

"Hey, your Master's back," Ryan said. "If he's into threesomes, let me know."

With a wink, Ryan went back to her previous seat.

Kimani watched Ben climb back into the boat, remove the ski vest and shake the water from his hair. He looked good wet.

Get a grip, Kimani.

Switching places, Derek took the driver's seat and Jake put on his ski vest. Ben headed in her direction.

CHAPTER EIGHTEEN

The water was still cool on his skin, helping to dampen the hard-on that threatened when he saw Kimani naked. He had enjoyed rubbing the sunblock all over her. Her arms, legs and back had felt almost as good as her ass and tits. She looked healthy yet supple. Womanly. Perfect.

"You want a turn?" he asked when he reached her.

"Turn?" she replied.

"Skiing."

"I don't know how."

"I can teach you."

She thought for a minute, then shook her head. "Maybe another time. When I have a swimsuit on."

"There's no one else out on the lake."

"Still."

He didn't push it and instead opened the cooler.

"I was wondering where the drinks were," Jason said.

Before tossing him a bottle of ale, Ben opened and handed bottles to all the women except for Kimani. Lisa yelped loudly when Jason ran the cold bottle over her belly.

"Let me guess—you want water," Ben said to Kimani.

She nodded. He grabbed two bottles of water, one for her, one for himself. She took the bottle, then raised her hand.

"Mind if I ask you something?"

"Go ahead."

"Do I have to ask permission to talk every time?"

He laughed. "That's your question?"

"Just need to know the ground rules."

Sitting down, he finished off half his bottle before replying, "No. That would get tedious."

"Do I have to call you Master all the time?"

It would be easier for her sake to set some consistent rules, but he didn't like sweating the small stuff.

"The more the merrier," he said, "but I'm not going to require you to do it every time. I'll let you know if that changes."

"Would you like your sunglasses back?"

"Keep them for now. They look good on you."

"I wouldn't want anything to happen to them. They seem like expensive glasses."

"They're just sunglasses. It's not like I can't get another pair."

"I'm so bad with sunglasses—losing them and scratching them up—that I only bother buying cheap ones. Once in a while I'll splurge and get a pair from Nordstrom Rack. Anyway, fair warning: your shades aren't safe with me."

"I'll take my chances."

She seemed to understand that his statement referred to more than sunglasses. After a brief awkward silence, she tossed her hair over her shoulders. He imagined sinking a fist into those curls and pulling her head back to expose her throat. Though he tried not to fix on her naked body, the tension in his groin was still tightening.

"So," she began, "you get off on making women display themselves as objects?"

She was trying to sound nonchalant and curious, but he detected an edge to her question. He passed his tongue over his lower lip as he contemplated how best to answer.

"I get off on seeing naked women. Given I'm not gay, there'd be something seriously wrong with me if I didn't. Don't you get off on seeing a guy naked?"

"Depends on the guy."

"Idris Elba."

"Well, sure. There'd be something seriously wrong with me if I didn't."

She was parroting his words back on purpose, as he had done to her.

"Then what's the problem, other than the fact that I'm not Idris Elba?"

She blinked several times—then laughed, a genuine non-nervous laugh. He liked it.

"No, you're not," she acknowledged, "but I guess it doesn't matter for you."

"That's right. Because when I want, I'll make you

forget all about Idris fucking Elba."

Her mouth was agape in that sexy way again, a little dumbfounded but not dumb.

"I don't think Idris Elba would make women sit around naked just for kicks."

"How do you know? Men aren't that complicated."

"Some men have evolved beyond caveman thinking — or lack thereof."

"A lot of women like cavemen."

"That's because they're not enlightened."

He raised his brows.

"I mean, maybe they don't know any better. No modern woman in her right mind wants a caveman who will club her over the head and drag her into his cave by her hair."

"You so sure about that?"

She glanced over at the other women. "I guess I shouldn't make generalizations, but for me and my friends, we're not looking for a lunkhead with big biceps whose penis is bigger than his brain. Maybe for *men*, it doesn't matter so much if the woman is a bimbo, as long as she'll suck his cock for him."

He pulled her toward him and pinned her with his gaze. "You don't think I can get cock-sucking bimbos for a lot less than two hundred thousand?"

Lowering her lashes, she avoided his look, murmuring, "I'm sure you can get cock-sucking bimbos for nothing."

"Now, just because you went to Stanford, it doesn't mean you can't be a bimbo. Some of the biggest idiots

I've ever met come from places like Stanford and Harvard."

"Do you consider me a bimbo?"

He released her. "I don't shell out two hundred thousand dollars for cock-sucking bimbos."

She wasn't buying it. "Oh, so you're not looking to have sex. You're interested in my intellect?"

He laughed. "I don't have a problem sleeping with not-so-intellectual women."

She shook her curls. "I knew it."

"Whoa. Before you cast stones, are you saying you'd only fuck a guy whose *intellectual*?"

"He has to be a good person, preferably smart and caring."

"Then how come you came so easily for me?"

She flushed. "I guess I figured you couldn't be all bad if you went to Howard."

"That's a dangerous generalization. I could still be a huge asshole."

Still holding his gaze, she lifted her chin, but there was a hint of appreciation curling the corners of her lips. "Yeah, you totally could."

He lowered his voice and repeated his question. "Then how come you came for me yesterday?"

When she didn't answer right away, he had to stay himself from pressing her. He was curious to know what she had to say. Their conversation should have stalled his ardor; instead, it was making him harder. And he wanted to go there.

"I guess the body has a mind of its own, so to

speak," she replied.

"And what happened to 'smart and caring'?"

"Are you saying you're not smart and caring?"

"Doesn't matter what I think. What were you thinking at the time you squirted into my hand?"

She thought for a moment. "If I thought you were a total dickwad, I wouldn't have come. Maybe some women are okay being felt up by strangers and assholes, but if some lech — billionaire or not — groped me, I'd want to punch him in the balls. See how he likes being touched in the privates without permission."

"That's an interesting perspective for someone who auctioned off her body."

"It's completely different. I *consented* to the auction. I *chose* to do it."

"So what would have happened if I had been a complete asshole?"

"I reserve the right to change my mind and drop out of the arrangement."

"But then you don't see a penny from the auction."

"I know. Plus, I'm out a 'processing fee' of two thousand dollars."

"That's pretty steep, assuming most of the women are participating because they need the money in a bad way."

"It is."

He scratched his chin. "So, you were betting on not being bought by an asshole? Not sure I would have taken those odds."

"Not a complete asshole," she retorted. "I figured

there would be some element of asshole-ness, or at least desperation, in all the buyers at the Scarlet Auction. Who else would need to buy a woman in the first place?"

He could have clarified that he didn't *need* to buy her. He just *wanted* to. Instead, he said, "Maybe it's the thought of owning a woman, even for a week, that makes it exciting."

"Last I checked, slavery ended with the Civil War in this country."

Some of his former classmates at Howard would disagree with her statement and argue that slavery was alive and well, just in more insidious forms that society wouldn't recognize as slavery. But he didn't want to get too deep into a scholarly debate.

"In BDSM, the bondage is titillating for the slave, too." And just to rile her up a little, he added, "You'll like being my slave."

Her breath seemed to stick in her throat. "You so sure about that?"

"I found the right buttons to push yesterday, didn't I?"

"That was yesterday. You weren't being as big an asshole."

Inwardly, he smiled. He had sensed, correctly, that she wasn't pleased with his decision to have her go naked like the other women.

Grabbing her by the arm, he yanked her to him and caught her jaw in his other hand. Leaning closer, he said low into her ear, "First of all, it's risky calling your

Master an asshole, even if I am one. Secondly…challenge accepted."

CHAPTER NINETEEN

Kimani maintained what she hoped was a cool exterior, but her toes curled at his nearness and gruff handling. She was not herself with this guy. When she should have been quiet or focused on asking questions to probe into his psyche, she found herself defensive and much too verbose with her own opinions. It was like all her training had gone out the door. She couldn't shut up and just do her job.

"What challenge?" she asked, her words coming out shakier than she wanted.

"You think you won't come for me today? I'm going to prove you wrong, pet. Over and over."

Jesus. How was she going to get herself out of this? Did she want to get herself out of it?

Jake had finished with his skiing and was back aboard the boat. Derek cut the engine, leaving them to float near the middle of the lake. When the two of them climbed to the front of the boat, Ben pulled her closer till she sat between his legs. Kimani didn't mind being as far away from Jake and Derek as possible, though feeling Ben's thighs pressed to hers rattled her more than she would have liked.

"You sluts having fun?" Derek asked after he plopped himself down beside Ryan with an open bottle of ale.

"Yes, Master," Ryan replied.

Jake settled into the seating next to Claire. "Why don't you sluts put on a show for us?"

"What kind of a show?"

"I like me a little girl-on-girl action. Let's do Slut #1 with Slut #3."

Claire looked a little bewildered. "Umm…"

"Maybe she's not up for that," Kimani said, and received a glare from Jake.

Claire nodded. "I'm not a…lesbian."

"I don't give a fuck," Jake said. "Nothing turns a guy on more than girl-on-girl. You want to please your Master, don't you?"

"Yes, Master."

Clearly more at ease, Ryan went to sit beside Claire.

"Now kiss," Jake ordered.

Ryan cupped Claire's face and brushed her lips over Claire's before pressing her mouth down more fully.

"Let's see some tongue."

The two women parted their lips and obliged.

"That is so hot," Jason exhaled.

"Now feel each other up."

Claire put a tentative hand to Ryan's breast. Ryan covered Claire's hand and squeezed.

Ben's chest grazed the back of her shoulder as he leaned in. He whispered in her ear, "What are you thinking?"

Depending on her answer, would he make her participate with Claire and Ryan?

"Do you really care what I think?" she deflected.

"Answer me."

"At the moment, I'm thinking…" *That Jake is a jerk.* "I'd rather not say in present company."

"You don't like that the women are being told what to do."

"Something like that."

"That's part of the appeal of BDSM. When you're told what to do, you're free."

"How's that?"

"Free of responsibility, free from having to think, free to enjoy the moment. The decision-making is on the dominant."

"What if you don't like how the dominant is handling his responsibility?"

"You tell him, or you lay out ahead of time what your hard and soft limits are. And if you don't know what they are, the dominant helps you explore them. He helps you step out of your comfort zone and try things you might not otherwise consider."

She couldn't help but wonder what limits Ben may have her explore.

"Oh, shit," Derek mumbled when Ryan dropped her head down to take Claire's nipple into her mouth.

"Does that turn you on at all?"

Claire looked a little less uncomfortable as their kissing and caressing continued.

"You ever kissed another woman?"

Kimani observed the softness of Claire and Ryan's bodies, the supple curves a stark contrast to the straight lines of a man.

"Once. In college, at a dorm party. I don't know why, maybe I was a little drunk, but Leticia and I started flirting."

She thought she heard a soft growl in the back of his throat.

"And then?"

"We kissed, nothing more because I knew I wasn't gay. I didn't want to lead her on."

"Have you thought about kissing a woman since then?"

"I've seen a few porn videos of woman making out."

"And did they turn you on?"

She wasn't sure why she was being so candid with him. Maybe she wanted the safety of their conversation.

"It's okay to admit that you were turned on," he said. "Men and women are conditioned to the sexualization of women. And the sight of women together is beautiful. Who better to worship a woman's asset than another woman?"

It was a rhetorical question, so she didn't answer. Ben threaded his fingers through her right hand, his touch always warm and firm. With their fingers entwined, he brought her hand to the base of her pelvis and smoothed the curls there.

"Now go down on her," Jake ordered Claire.

Claire balked, scrunching up her nose. But Ryan willingly lay down and spread her legs.

"Come on now. Don't keep me waiting."

Claire lowered her body, settling her shoulders between Ryan's thighs.

"Get a good whiff of her snatch. How does it smell?"

"Umm...okay," responded Claire.

Ben pushed one of her fingers between her folds to stroke her clitoris. The memory of last night slammed into her. They sat a little ways from the rest of the group, but she wasn't comfortable being aroused in front of everyone. Not that anyone was paying attention to her. Jake was busy directing Claire. Lisa and Jason were making out again. Derek had pulled his erection from his swim trunks and was giving himself a hand job.

"Play with yourself," Ben said. "Get that clit nice and big."

Together, they stroked her sensitive nub of flesh before he disengaged his fingers from hers. She stopped.

"Keep going," he urged, "or I'll make you take Claire's place."

Her breath hitched. Would he really make her do that? She had a safety word, which he'd said he would honor. But rather than testing him, she resumed stroking herself on her own.

"That's a good pet."

She could feel his hardness pressing against her

backside. Lisa was making all kinds of noises, gasps and little high-pitched cries. Now Ryan joined in with her moans. Derek jerked himself faster.

Ben entwined his fingers with her free hand and brought it to her breast, compelling her to feel herself up.

"Would you rather be Claire or Ryan at this moment?" he asked.

"Ryan."

"Why?"

"Because she looks like she's enjoying herself."

"You sure you wouldn't want to be Claire? Being made to do something you've never done before, maybe something you think is wrong and embarrassing, and because it's wrong and embarrassing, it's fucking erotic?"

Kimani swallowed with difficulty. "I'm not so sure Claire thinks of it that way."

"What would *you* think? How would you feel if you were the one licking another woman's pussy? Do you have a secret desire to try it? What if I made you do it, and punished you if you didn't?"

Did he want answers or was he just provoking her?

"Imagine it."

She gasped when his hand, still on top of hers, forced her to squeeze her breast. Kimani closed her eyes, preferring not to see Jake, who had positioned Claire on her knees, inserting himself from behind. She pictured herself in Claire's place, between Ryan's thighs. Could she go down on another woman? Would she want to? Maybe not in real life because she didn't know Ryan well enough, but maybe in a fantasy? Sometimes the fantasy was more titillating than reality.

"Are you imagining it?" Ben asked, his voice low and husky.

She nodded, then started when his forefinger joined hers, teasing her clit. His finger dipped lower and connected with wetness. How had that happened? Maybe it was the sights, sounds and scents of arousal all around her. It was contagious.

What was that challenge he had mentioned?

When he touched her like that, she couldn't think straight. So much for being enlightened. Maybe she wasn't so different from the other women?

No, she was different. Because she wasn't here for sex or money or to realize some fictional romance. She was here to get the scoop on the sordid world of the Scarlet Auction. And in order to do that, she just had to find a way to get back on that cliff.

CHAPTER TWENTY

To Ben's disappointment, her body tensed, but not in a good way. With her wedged between his legs, her back resting against him, he had sensed it all too easily. She had been succumbing to arousal, losing her inhibitions in present company, but some thought had run through her head, interrupting the more primal desires of her body.

His hardened cock was going crazy being so near her without penetrating, but he wasn't going to give up easily. He was looking forward to proving her wrong.

"Hey, how about we have Slut #2 and #4 take a turn putting on a show?" Jake asked as he thrust his hips into Claire, who was bent over and still trying to attend to Ryan.

Claire and Ryan were a pretty sight, but nowhere near as hot as the vision of Kimani going down on another woman. For a brief moment, Ben entertained the idea.

"I like my pet where she is," he replied. If he was going to make Kimani perform oral sex, it was not going to be because Jake wanted it.

Jason let out a loud grunt as he came with Lisa

sitting atop him. He shook as if having a seizure. Derek followed shortly after, and Jake went back to pounding Claire to seek his own release. Claire wasn't able to keep up with the cunnilingus, so Ryan took matters into her own hand, literally.

"Do you want to come, too?" Ben asked softly to Kimani.

"I'm fine," she replied.

She didn't sound completely fine, but he let it go. After Jake finished, most of the men lay in a post-coital stupor. Claire nestled herself next to Jake, a pensive look on her face. Lisa was examining her nails. Ben shook his head. He'd have to have a talk with Jason about pleasuring women.

Turning back to Kimani, he placed his leg, bent, on the seating, pulling her leg along, spreading her. She gasped.

"What's the matter?" he asked.

"It's…people…" she replied, trying to set her leg back down.

But he held her in place. "You're fingering yourself, and they can see."

Ryan was rubbing herself furiously and making enough noise to draw everyone's attention.

"Don't tell me you've never exposed your pussy?" Ben asked.

"To boyfriends and my gynecologist."

"So you've never had group sex?"

"No."

"Witnessed it?"

"I've seen a lot of people make out, especially in college, at parties. My freshman-year roommate had a lot of boyfriends. They sometimes slept over, and I would wake up in the middle of the night to hear them going at it. But I didn't *look.* I'd rather—maybe when we're back in the cabin—"

"Shhh. I want you to close your eyes."

She hesitated.

"It's going to be a long night if you don't obey the simple orders."

She pursed her lips but complied, closing her eyes.

He continued to guide her fingers, stroking her clit as he asked the next question. "Have you had any other voyeuristic experiences?"

"Aside from watching porn or reading erotica?"

He was glad to hear she watched porn. Not many women allowed themselves that activity. "What kind of porn do you watch?"

"Nothing in particular, just free stuff on the Internet."

"Tell me about it."

"They're not that memorable."

He pinched her clit, making her gasp. "If you don't remember, you can make one up for me."

"I remember one of them was a threesome."

"What kind of threesome? MFM?"

"More like M, F, and hermaphrodite."

Interesting.

"Was it hot?"

"Yeah… it was."

"What was the hottest part?"

"It was the first time I had seen double penetration of one, um, orifice. I had never considered it a possibility before."

"Ever have it done to you?"

She shook her head. Her breath was uneven, and he felt moisture building below her clit.

"Would you like to?"

She opened her eyes and glanced at the guys on the boat. "No."

"Keep your eyes closed. What if the circumstances were right? Like, you're locked in a room with Idris Elba and his twin?"

She laughed a little nervously. "Okay, I guess I'd give it a try."

"Did you imagine how it would feel to have two cocks stretching your pussy?"

"It's probably easier said than done."

"It's not as hard as you think."

"You've done it before?" she inquired, sounding genuinely curious.

"A few times."

He dipped a finger into her nectar and spread it over her clitoris, which had swelled in size. She squirmed a little.

"Tell me what kind of sex you like," he said.

"Um, the good kind."

"You don't like to be specific." He thought about asking her what was on the Scarlet Auction questionnaire, then decided, "That's okay. It's going to be more fun to find out for myself."

Her chest rose as she inhaled sharply. Ryan emitted a groan when she came. Hearing, seeing, and even smelling the sex all around them was making his hard-on supremely uncomfortable. He had Kimani in his arms, one hand over a breast, the other toying with her clit. God, what he wouldn't do to be able to pick her up and sit her down on his knob.

"Your turn to come," he told her.

"I—"

He stroked with her, their fingers sliding next to each other, until she had crossed the point from which retreat would be too agonizing. Gradually, he disengaged his hand from between her thighs to grab her other breast.

"That's it," he coaxed. "You're too fucking hot not to come."

Slumped against him, she continued to ply her clitoris. She had been more vocal last night, but little grunts and pants escaped her lips. He rolled and squeezed her breasts. The things he wanted to do to her...

Would have to wait. With a wavering moan, she began to shudder. Her head fell back as she arched before she relaxed against him. Her fingers slowed to a crawl, and she exhaled a contented sigh.

He kissed her temple, surprising himself with the tender peck. "Good pet."

Though a part of him wanted to get back to the cabin as soon as possible so he could toss her onto the bed and pound away at that hot and wet pussy, he stayed where he was, soaking in the warmth of her cradled against him.

"I'm hungry," declared Derek.

"I haven't even gotten to my second bottle," Jake complained after making his way to the cooler.

"I'll fucking drive then."

Derek climbed into the driver's seat and started the engine. As the boat cut through the water, Ben wondered what he should do with Kimani next. He had refrained from pointing out that she had come for him again, but he wasn't done proving his point.

Coming to, she sat up and no longer seemed comfortable near him. He wanted to grab her back to him, pass his hands all over her body, but he let her have some space.

When they were back in the cabin, Jake barked out his next order. "Make us some lunch, sluts."

"I can make some sandwiches, maybe a salad," Ryan said before turning to Kimani. "Can you take care of dinner?"

"Sure," Kimani answered. She turned to Ben. "Can I borrow your cellphone now?"

He handed her his phone. Like yesterday, she went into the bathroom to make her call.

He motioned for Jason to join him out on the patio. They stood at the railing overlooking the lake.

"You know how to get a woman to come, don't you?" he asked Jason.

Jason did a double take. "Sure."

"It didn't look like Lisa came."

"Well... It's not like she's my girlfriend. She's getting paid to get laid."

"So?"

"It's a lot of work. That's what's so cool about the Scarlet Auction. The women aren't high maintenance."

"You might find Lisa a lot more enthusiastic if you threw her a bone, and not just your boner. Don't you *want* her more enthusiastic? Wouldn't you want a woman to ride your cock like there's no tomorrow? Or do you prefer to pound pussy while the woman is lying there comatose, counting the seconds for it to be over?"

"I guess...but some women take forever to come."

"Stop being such a wuss. Man up. And try lasting longer."

"Sorry if I'm not a sex god like you."

"When I first started out, I could barely last more than five minutes. Stamina is something you build."

"Okay, okay. You sure know how to take the fun out of things."

Ben shook his head. It was like talking to a petulant little boy.

Turning around, Jason leaned his back against the railing. "So did you find a good prospect from Jake?"

"I'm setting up a meeting next week with Tyrell Jenkins out of UCLA. While I'm down there, I'm going to round up some donations for Uncle Gordon. Want to come with?"

Jason made a face. "I'm not interested in political

stuff. Bad enough my dad wants me to pass out flyers and shit."

"If Uncle Gordon gets elected, we have a good shot at getting that waterfront land deal."

"Yeah, yeah, but it's not like we don't have enough to do. If I have to work in the family business, I'd rather do that hotel in Thailand you're working on."

"Maybe I can work something out."

"Thanks. Your dad will probably overrule it, though. He thinks I'm a total flake."

"You are. Because you've got potential and would rather sit on your arse. But if you're interested, I'll talk to my dad."

"Sure."

They said nothing for a few minutes, and Ben realized that Kimani was still in the bathroom. He went to see if she was still on her call.

"Really?" he heard her say through the bathroom door. "Mayor of Oakland? The family is into everything… Sure, let me know what else you find. … You really think this could be big? … Okay, talk to you tomorrow."

Why was she interested in Uncle Gordon, Ben wondered? And what did she mean by "this could be big?"

The bathroom door opened, and she looked startled to see him. She handed him his cellphone.

"Thanks for letting me use it again."

"Is Sam satisfied that you're okay?"

"Yeah, but she wants a call again tomorrow. Do

you mind if I put a shirt on? The AC is blasting in here."

He nodded, then went upstairs to his room to make a phone call of his own.

"With the cell number you gave me, our contact in Singapore turned up a Samuel Green," Stephens reported. "He's the editor-in-chief of the *San Francisco Tribune*. Before that, he was at the Pacific Institute for Investigative Reporting. Currently lives in San Francisco, Haight-Ashbury. Has a husband, Kyle Santos, and two kids."

Ben was quiet as he let the information sink in. So, Sam wasn't a woman, and if he was gay and married, then he wasn't likely to be Kimani's boyfriend or lover. What was he then? Her boss?

"I want you to look up a woman, age twenty-five. African-American," Ben said. "Graduate of Stanford with a BA in Communications. Lives in San Francisco."

"You got a name?"

"I've got a first name: Kimani."

THE END

HIS FOR A WEEK: RAVAGED

(available June 2018)

EXCERPT

CHAPTER ONE

I *can't keep screwing up like this.*

It didn't help to beat herself up over something that was over and done with, but Kimani had never been in a situation like this before. She was supposed to be working — undercover. Which meant that she had be extra careful not to compromise the story or its subjects. And her own journalistic integrity.

What had she done instead?

Become sexually involved with one of the subjects. And not just any subject. Beside her in the driver seat of the Jeep Wrangler sat the son of one of the wealthiest families in the world. When he took over the family business, Benjamin Dimitri Lee would be worth somewhere in the vicinity of twelve billion dollars.

Her editor, Sam Green, hadn't wasted any time. With the bits of information she had provided him last night — an Asian named Ben who went to Howard University, then the Stanford business school and was recruiting for a team in the Chinese Basketball Association — he had come back with the Lee Family Corporation. Ben's father, Lee Hua Jing, had founded the Lee Family Corporation, making his first million in residential real estate before branching into commercial real estate and investments of all kinds. Mr. Lee's younger brother, Gordon, had immigrated to the United States as a teenager when the family was still struggling to make ends meet and was now in a tightly contested election for Mayor of Oakland. And one of the hot button issues in the election was the development of a piece of waterfront property that the Lee Family Corporation had shown interest in.

"This could be a great scoop," Sam had said. "You've got to find out more."

But Benjamin Lee was a tangent. A tall, sexy tangent whose sensuous touch had a way of shutting down her brain. Even now, she tried not to glance over to admire how his simple shirt fit luxuriously over his broad shoulders and chiseled chest. She supposed this was a side effect of not having had sex in the last six months because she was focused on her career trying to land a job for *The San Francisco Tribune*.

She was supposed to be reporting on the Scarlet Auction, where women sold themselves for a week to the highest bidder. Undercover, Kimani had participated in the auction with the intent of exposing its sordid business. Ben hadn't attended the actual auction, but he had "bought" her from the man, a sports agent named Jake, who had won her with a bid of thirty thousand dollars.

It was crazy shit that had boggled Kimani's mind. Jake's first purchase, a blonde virgin named Claire, had "sold" for eighty thousand dollars. But crazy went through the stratosphere when Ben offered Jake two hundred thousand dollars.

Kimani couldn't fathom why he would shell out that kind of money for her unless (a) two hundred thousand dollars was just the equivalent of a pricey vacation and he could easily make the amount back if the HKEX had a good run, (b) Ben didn't want to be the only guy in the group without a date — correction: fucktoy — or (c) Ben was messed up in the head somehow.

But he didn't seem irrational or deranged. In fact, out of all the people she was stuck in a lakeside cabin in the boonies of Northern California with, he seemed the most calm and collected. Even now, when they had been driving in silence for several minutes, she could sense him looking at her, at ease with their silence, probably wondering what she was thinking but restrained enough not to ask.

Her American-style impatience got the better of her, however, and she turned to ask him, "Where are we going?"

For a second, she wondered if psychos had the capability of appearing completely normal. He had put the top down on the Jeep Wrangler, and if he had intended to drive her somewhere with evil intentions, he wouldn't have wanted himself and his victim to be so visible, right? Then again, they were in one of the least populated counties in the state. Trinity County was mostly rugged, heavily forested wilderness.

"We're going into Weaverville to get you some clothes," he replied.

His answer surprised her. This morning he had made her go onto Jake's boat without a shred of clothing. Afterwards, he had allowed her to put on the cocktail dress, her only clothing item, with his shirt over it. She hadn't had a chance to wash the sweats he had lent her. Remembering that she didn't have on panties, she pressed her legs together.

"I don't have any money with me," she said. Her cellphone and her wallet had disappeared from her handbag sometime after the auction had concluded and before she had been ushered into a limo that had driven her and Claire straight to Jake's cabin. Ben had let her use his cellphone twice, and it was her only connection to the rest of the world. Sam knew she was somewhere near Weaverville because that's all she knew. And that probably wasn't going to be helpful if things should turn ugly.

"You don't need any money."

"Oh. I'll pay you back when we get back to San Francisco."

'When' we get back. Not 'if.' She had had her worries yesterday, especially after Jake had hit her before Ben had arrived. Ben had been her savior buying her from Jake because the thought of laying a finger on Jake made her want to retch. Even though she barely knew him, she felt safe with Ben.

Relatively safe, she cautioned herself. Ben had an edge. She could see it when his pupils constricted and his jaw tightened. Beneath that cool exterior lay a tiger. He kept a good leash on it, but she couldn't be sure what would set it off.

"I've got it," he said.

"I'd rather pay you back."

"Maybe if you're a good pet, I'll let you pay me back."

She bristled at the word 'pet.' It was better than being called 'Slut #2,' Jake's original moniker for her, but not that much better.

"I insist."

He glanced at her as if she were a child who wanted to have cookies before bed. "You don't get to make the rules, pet."

She bristled again. "Then maybe I don't want to get any clothes."

As soon as the words escaped her mouth, she regretted her childish response. It was an outright lie. She wanted something other than her cocktail dress and clothes borrowed from him, even though his shirt and sweatpants were the softest things she had ever worn. She wanted underwear. Desperately. Having a shield of any kind down there might help reign those carnal instincts from running away with her better judgment.

She had said what she said because she wanted some small sliver of control, and she didn't want to be beholden to Ben more than she already was.

But Ben granted her no concessions. "You're welcome to go naked the whole week."

Then maybe I don't want to stay the whole week.

This time she curbed herself from saying anything rash. Ben had said he wasn't going to force her to stay and had even offered to fly her back to San Francisco in his jet. He had sounded sincere. But she didn't have enough material for her story. And she couldn't abandon Claire to Jake. He might be as bad as the man who had beaten up Kimani's roommate.

"I'll find a way to pay you back," Kimani decided aloud. Maybe she'd make a donation in his name to the ACLU or the local Black Women's Political Caucus. Maybe then he'd prefer to take her money.

He gave her an amused look but said nothing as they neared Weaverville. With the Trinity Alps as its backdrop, Weaverville was a picturesque Gold Rush town. Though the last census pegged the population at less than four thousand people, the main street looked busy, probably from the influx of tourists taking advantage of the area's outdoor sports offerings.

The clothing retail options were limited, but Ben found a thrift store to park in front of. He left her alone to peruse the clothing racks. She found a tank top, t-shirt, a long knit skirt that went almost to her ankles, a pair of khaki shorts, a sports bra, flip-flops, a silk scarf to tie her hair up at night, and cheap sunglasses so that she could return Ben his Louis Vutton shades. At the checkout, Ben had a few items to purchase as well: candles, clothespins and a set of chopsticks. She wondered what the clothespins were for. Surely he wasn't planning to do laundry at the cabin?

Eager to be out of her heels and strange ensemble, she changed into the shirt, shorts and flip-flops and immediately felt better. Now she only needed underwear.

As if reading her mind, Ben said, "There's a CVS store about a mile down."

"Can we walk?" she asked. The summer sun shone warmly, and she preferred taking in the downtown scenery with its many 19th century buildings to going back to the cabin where Jake and his buddies were.

After putting their purchase in the car, they started walking down Main Street. She had never been in this part of the state before. Her eyes lighted upon seeing a sign for the Joss House State Historic Park.

Ben didn't miss much. "You want to check it out?"
"Definitely!"

While on Jake's boat earlier today, upset that Ben
had her go naked like the other three women, she had
insinuated he was an asshole. But moments like this
showed he couldn't be a complete asshole. This and the
fact that he had let her take a nap in his room yesterday
afternoon and had looked upset to see the basement
where Jake had her and the other "sluts" sleep. Ben
had made sure she and Claire had had something to
eat when they were hungry after being made by Jake
to kneel on the floor for three hours. And, despite
having made her come twice yesterday and once
today, he had yet to ask or demand she return the
favor. He had made no bones about the fact that he had
purchased her for sex, so why hadn't he made her do
anything? Maybe he was embarrassed about his size
down there? Somehow, she doubted that was what
was holding him back. When she felt more generously
inclined toward him, she thought that perhaps he just
wanted to make her comfortable. But surely that was
giving him too much credit? After all, he had paid
money—a ridiculous amount of money—for sex. He
couldn't be that different from the other overgrown
frat boys: Jake, Derek, and Jason.

Turning the corner, they came upon a quaint red
building. Built in 1874 and dubbed "The Temple of the
Forest Beneath the Clouds," the Weaverville Joss
House was the oldest Chinese Temple in California.
Weaverville was once home to some 2,000 Chinese
gold miners. Many Chinese immigrants came to
California in the nineteenth century for the state's

famed Gold Rush or to work as laborers on the transcontinental railroad. Their large numbers caused Congress to pass the Chinese Exclusion Act, the only US law ever to prevent immigration and naturalization on the basis of race.

The interior housed displays of art, pictures, mining tools and weapons used in the 1854 Tong war.

"A friend of mine carried a small hatchet similar to this one," said Ben, almost to himself.

"Why would he carry around a hatchet?" Kimani asked.

"He was old-fashioned. Didn't like guns because they were a Western invention."

"Gunpowder was a Chinese invention, though I guess it was the Europeans who used it for mass destruction and guns. Was your friend extremely paranoid? Or was carrying around a hatchet some kind of alpha guy thing?"

"Chen Kai wasn't more paranoid than the rest of us."

"Rest of us?"

"When I was young and my father was busy taking the family business to the next level, I started getting into gangs. That's why he shipped me off to boarding school in London."

"Were you pretty deep in a gang?"

"I didn't kill anyone if that's what you're worried about."

It was sort of what worried her. "So what did you do in the gang?"

"Not much since I was still pretty young at the time. Stupid boy shit. Probably got myself beat up more than anything else."

She had a hard time imagining anyone beating up on Ben. She saw how he moved. Smooth like a ballerina, flowing like one of those dragons in the Chinese New Year's Parade. She had seen him in nothing but his swim trunks. His muscles were well defined everywhere, not in a beefy way but plenty delicious for her to want to run her hands over the planes and ridges of his chest and torso.

"Did you have to carry a weapon?" she asked.

"I carried a knife and learned how to make myself a weapon through martial arts. The gang was small potatoes, only loosely connected to one of the triads but enough to worry my dad."

She itched to ask him a dozen questions, which she would have done if she were openly interviewing him, but since she wasn't, everything was technically off record. She wanted to know anyway but didn't want to appear prying.

They walked to the area of worship.

"This is so cool," she whispered of the paper prayers on the walls and intricately carved altars decorated with bold colors of red and gold. "It's not something I expected to find out here."

She looked at one of the scrolls hanging from beside the altar. "Do you read?"

After he had translated the Chinese on the scrolls, which talked of the emperor, gods, and devils, she recalled, "One of my dormmates at Stanford claimed to be a Taoist, but he only talked about it in reference to sex. I'm not sure how authentic it all was. Some people thought he was just being an 'egg.'"

She glanced at him, and it was like walking into a brick wall when she met his stare. At first, she thought maybe he didn't like that she had used the term 'egg' since it was sometimes used in a critical manner to refer to white Asiaphiles, but there was an amused gleam in Ben's dark brown eyes that told her he was fixed on *her*, not her words. She could barely swallow. He looked as if he had some secret he may or may not share with her. She wanted to know what it was, even though she was certain that finding out would only get her deeper in trouble.

CHAPTER TWO

B y her expression, not unlike a deer caught in headlights, Ben supposed he must have been staring at Kimani like she was a piece of meat he wanted to devour. And he did. On the drive over to Weaverville, he had toyed with the idea of pulling over and making her come all over the car. He was going to make her squirt again, just like he had the night before. The morning swim through the lake's cold waters had helped clear his head, but spending all that time on the boat and seeing her naked had put him back to square one. Her body had felt so damn good leaning against his.

She stood inches from him looking like a frumpy tourist with her broad-brimmed hat, cheap sunglasses, and khaki shorts. And if there had been no one around, he would have been tempted to rip her clothes off and take her right there in the temple. Or at least feel her up through the thin tank top she wore. He had noticed she had chosen a sports bra, which made her breasts less accessible, but she was wrong if she thought a little sports bra could protect her.

"Sex is an important part of Taoism," he explained, "and some engage in intercourse as part of a spiritual practice."

"Really? Sex is usually taboo and *wrong* when it comes to religions."

"Taoism isn't a religion in the same way as Catholicism or Judaism. It's a philosophy and a way of living. Central to Taoist practice is the care and cultivation of *jing*, essence or energy. Sex is the joining of this energy."

She was eying him curiously, as if trying to read his mind. If she could, she would see herself spent and exhausted as he wrung yet another orgasm from her. She had no idea how long a session with him could last. Most women couldn't keep up, and he wondered how Kimani would fare compared to the others.

"That sounds very holistic, spiritual," she commented. Then, as if sensing his thoughts, though she couldn't see them, she turned and stepped away. "Looks like there's a garden out back."

A deer leaped over the fence as they strolled outside and to a fountain with a small statue of Kuan Yin.

"'One who listens,'" Kimani read from the plaque in front of the fountain. "Is she a goddess?"

"Sort of. She is an enlightenment being and the gateway to a paradise where souls are reborn with the truth of their eternal nature, compassion and joy."

"That sounds lovely. You seem to know quite a bit about Taoism."

He didn't tell her that it was the Taoist sex practices that had been his primary interest. It was best to stay away from topics of a sexual nature. Any wood would show in his tight-fitting jeans.

Instead, he said "Taoism is embedded in Chinese

culture, though much of it was suppressed in favor of Confucianism."

After they finished their visit at the Joss House, he decided to stop in one of the coffee shops to get something to drink. He wanted Kimani to himself and was in no hurry to get back to the cabin where his cousin, Jason, was probably getting stoned with Tweedle-Dee and Tweedle-Dum. The three of them had tried to convince him to attend the Scarlet Auction to "buy" a woman for the week. He had thought the idea of "buying" a woman stupid—for guys too lazy to get real dates. But the instant he saw Kimani, he had to have her. Or at least he couldn't let Jake keep her, especially if he was the one that had given her the bruise on her cheek, which had deepened in hue since yesterday.

If it weren't for the fact that Jake Whitehurst represented players that the coach of the Golden Phoenix wanted to recruit to play in the Chinese Basketball Association, Ben would not have chosen to spend the week in the wilderness of Northern California. But Kimani was going to make it all worthwhile.

At the coffee shop, he ordered two mugs of green tea.

"Green tea?" Kimani echoed in disbelief. "It's warm out here. I was hoping to get an iced mocha."

"Green tea is healthier."

"So is broccoli juice but that doesn't mean I want to drink it."

Should he tell her that green tea enhances *physical performance* or would that scare her off?

"Do you only do what you want?" he returned, taking the mugs of tea from the barrista.

She followed him to a table. "Of course not. I'm not a child. But...green tea? *Hot* green tea on a sunny afternoon?"

"You'll get used to it."

She gave him a small glare as she sat down. He almost laughed when she grimaced into her tea.

"You can have a glass of water after you've had some of your tea," he said.

She blew at the tea to cool it down. "You're obnoxious."

"We established earlier that I was an asshole," he acknowledged before leaning in and lowering his voice. "You came for me anyway."

She flushed. "Well, that's because you're not a *complete* asshole. Just partly. Maybe a majority. I haven't decided yet."

He leaned back in his chair with his tea. She was cute when she was flustered. He knew her type: smart, well-educated, a little arrogant. But she had enough humility inside of her that if she were knocked down from her high horse, she would get up stronger and wiser.

"So what is it you exactly do? Do you work for the Chinese Basketball Association?" she asked.

"You haven't had any of your tea yet," he told her.

As he watched her take a sip, he smiled to himself. She was trainable.

"Is that why you're doing business with Jake?"

He nodded at her tea. "Drink more."

She took another sip. "So do you?"

"Why are you so interested?"

"Curious. I used to play," she reminded him. "A part of me wishes I was good enough to play professionally."

"How do you know you aren't?"

"I guess if I had tried—but when I was applying to college, the WNBA was struggling, so it wasn't clear what options I would have playing ball. But I like what I'm doing now."

He raised a brow. "Working as an office assistant?"

She looked down. "I know that's not what most Stanford grads aspire to, but it pays the bills."

"Does it? You wouldn't have done the Scarlet Auction if you had enough money."

"Right. I meant my job pays most of the bills. The Scarlet Auction is a great opportunity to make extra cash to pay off student loans and maybe have some fun."

"What does 'fun' entail?"

"Getting tickets to a Warriors game."

"Is that your favorite team?"

"The Stanford women's team is my favorite team, but the Warriors are a close second." She was smiling and looking more relaxed. She even took another sip of tea without prompting. "You didn't answer my question about working for the CBA."

"I don't work for the CBA. My father sponsors the Golden Phoenix, and it's his pet project to make the team into a championship contender."

"So when you're not working on that, what do you do?"

"Mostly real estate developments for the family

business."

"Any here in California?"

"Some."

"Like in the Bay Area?"

"Some."

He set down his now empty mug. Unlike most dates, she seemed interested in details. But this wasn't a date, even though it was beginning to feel like one. He didn't date because he wasn't looking to start a family.

"Are they commercial or residential?"

"These days policymakers like to see mixed-use."

"Do you like mixed-use?"

"If the pro forma works, sure. Mixed use is key to smart growth principles."

Her brows went up. "You care about smart growth?"

"Why shouldn't I?"

"I thought…"

"Thought what? That developers are evil and have no conscience when it comes to the environment? That we just care about maxing returns and triple net?"

"What's triple net?"

"It's a lease agreement in which the tenant agrees to pay the three 'nets' on the property: taxes, insurance and maintenance."

She seemed to be storing away that bit of information. He was surprised to find himself talking about lease agreements with any woman who wasn't in the business, but he believed few subjects would intimidate Kimani. And he found he talked rather freely with her. Hell, he had even revealed he had once hung with a gang. He couldn't remember the last person he had told that to.

Noting that she still had half a mug full, he told her, "Finish the tea."

She looked him in the eyes. "What if I don't want to?"

He returned a tight smile. "You sure you want to find out, pet?"

She pursed her lips but lifted the mug. "I'm drinking it because I know it's good for me."

He didn't bother disputing her. If the mug had root beer, she would be drinking it because he had told her to.

After the coffee shop, they walked to the drugstore where she found a package of Hanes underwear, various hair products, toiletries, a notepad, and pens.

"I'll pay you back," she said as the cashier rang everything up.

"I got it," he reminded her.

"I'd rather pay you back. It's all stuff I would have needed at home anyway."

He studied her, wondering why she insisted on paying him back when she was financially desperate enough to participate in the Scarlet Auction.

"You'll pay me back," he assured her, "just not in the way you think."

Her lips parted ever so slightly in a frown, and he had to look away before the urge to kiss her took over. As an Asian male and black female, they had received a handful of curious looks about town. He wasn't going to give them more to gawk at.

"I need something from the hardware store," he

said when they were done at CVS.

She followed him the few blocks and watched him peruse the different ropes available. He looked first at a solid polypropylene braid. It was soft and smooth to the touch and had solidity and weight. But the thickness would make for large knots, so he went for the twisted nylon, which was also soft and smooth. It wasn't as good as jute, but it would have to do. The white nylon would be a nice contrast against her skin.

"What's the rope for?" Kimani asked.

He raised his brows. "You don't know?"

She hesitated. "Is it for the boat?"

"I think you know what it's for: paying me back."

His For A Week:
RAVAGED

As billionaire Ben Lee inches closer to the truth, how long can undercover journalist Kimani Taylor continue her charade before his wicked seduction gets the better of her?

Ben:
I've been patient with her. Now it's my turn to take the pleasure I paid for when I bought her.

I'm not going to just use her. I'm going to *ravage* her.

Lightning Source UK Ltd.
Milton Keynes UK
UKHW020619050320
359822UK00011B/849

9 781942 822585